UNCHARTED
WATERS

For Julia and Isabel with love.
—L. B.

Ω

Published by
PEACHTREE PUBLISHERS
1700 Chattahoochee Avenue
Atlanta, Georgia 30318-2112

www.peachtree-online.com

Text © 2006 by Leslie Bulion

Jacket photograph of a Portuguese man-of-war © 2006 Peter Parks/
imagequestmarine.com

First trade paperback edition printed in 2009

Cover design by Loraine M. Joyner
Book design by Melanie McMahon Ives

Printed in the United States of America
10 9 8 7 6 5 4 3 2 (hardcover)
10 9 8 7 6 5 4 3 2 1 (trade paperback)

Library of Congress Cataloging-in-Publication Data

Bulion, Leslie, 1958-
  Uncharted waters / by Leslie Bulion.-- 1st ed.
    p. cm.
  Summary: Jonah's lies and his secret fear of the sea threaten to ruin his month at the shore with his favorite uncle, but a grumpy marina storekeeper and an attractive young college student help turn the summer into an adventure he will never forget.
  ISBN 13: 978-1-56145-365-8 / ISBN 10: 1-56145-365-X (hardcover)
  ISBN 13: 978-1-56145-485-3 / ISBN 10: 1-56145-485-0 (trade paperback)
  [1. Honesty--Fiction. 2. Swimming--Fiction. 3. Boats and boating--Fiction. 4. Mechanics--Fiction. 5. Brothers and sisters--Fiction. 6. Uncles--Fiction. 7. Authorship--Fiction. 8. Seashore--Fiction.] I. Title.
  PZ7.B911155Unc 2006
  [Fic]--dc22
                          2005028574

UNCHARTED
WATERS

Leslie Bulion

PEACHTREE
ATLANTA

Acknowledgments

I would like to thank the entire GSO and CRC community of 1979–1983 for their support, learning, and camaraderie, all of which persisted even when the scallop population didn't. Manifold thanks for the more recent, patient tutelage and careful manuscript checking by the original Toolboy, Jerry Milmoe, on all things boat and motor. Thanks also to Jerry Theise for his boat-guy expertise. Any similarities between the antics of Uncle Nate and those of Uncle Pete are not coincidental.

Thanks to my wonderful community of readers and supporters—my family and friends, the SCBWI CT Shoreline chapter, my hot Hot Toddies, Steven Chudney, and the family of editors at Peachtree. Special thanks to Vicky Holifield for her enthusiasm, and for her gentle, true, and deft eye and ear at each stage in the process of turning this rough story into a real live book.

CHAPTER ONE

N ow I've got you in my power!" Uncle Nate rubbed his hands together, rolled his eyes around in his head, and let out a diabolical laugh. "Bwa-ha-ha-ha!"

He hooked Jonah's and Jaye's bags over his arms and shoulders and dragged himself up the steps and into his cabin in an exaggerated limp. He let the screen door bang on his foot.

"Ahhhh!" he yelled. "I mean, bwa-ha-ha-ha!" He pulled his leg inside.

Jonah's younger sister Jaye folded her arms. "Very funny, Uncle Nate," she said. "Let's go swimming."

Any one of Jonah's city friends would gladly have traded a birthday to spend a single afternoon with Uncle Nate, let alone half the summer. His uncle was the biggest thirty-one-year-old kid Jonah knew. Six feet tall at least. When his uncle came to visit, kids collected on the stoop, drawn by the way he could conjure goofy games out of thin air.

Two years ago Jonah and his family had spent winter break at the ski resort his uncle managed. He'd taught them all to ski, but the best part was when he'd shown them, over and over again, the "right" way to fall. By the end of his demonstration, Uncle Nate's hair, eyebrows, shoulders, and every other body part had been coated with snow. He'd even had snow in his mouth. Jonah still laughed every time he remembered it. They'd called him "the abominable snow uncle" for a long time after that. Uncle Nate was full of energy, but even better, he was full of ideas. And his ideas were always fun. Maybe that's what makes Uncle Nate a good writer, Jonah thought. Well, a good, *struggling* writer, as Mom called him.

But right now Jonah wasn't thinking about having fun. Jonah had arrived at Uncle Nate's cabin in Rhode Island with trouble weighing him down, and the trouble wasn't just his relentless ten-year-old sister.

"I want to go swimming," Jaye said again.

"Why don't you go ask Uncle Nate?" Jonah suggested. "Maybe he didn't hear you the other twenty-three times."

"Hey, guys!" their uncle called from the cabin. "Come on in. You can stow your stuff and then we can—*oof!* What's in this blue duffel bag, cement blocks?"

"That's probably Jonah's toolbox," Jaye answered, bounding up the wooden steps. The screen door banged shut behind her. "I want to—"

"Go swimming," Jonah muttered.

He shook his head and looked down the narrow dirt road. The sharp, heavy smell of the salt pond tickled the back of his throat. All that was left of Mom, Dad, and the family station wagon was a hovering cloud of sandy dust. Jonah thought he could still hear a faint, uneven sputter in the distance. He wished he'd had time to check under the hood of the car before his parents left. He could've cleaned the spark plugs and adjusted the carburetor. Jonah sighed. There'd be no motor to tinker with here. Uncle Nate was, as he'd put it, "between cars."

His parents' old clunker was probably running fine, anyway. It wasn't as if they had to drive it all the way to Europe. They were going to fly there on a plane and have a great time. And their plan had been for Jonah to come here to Uncle Nate's and have a great time, too.

He put his hands into his pockets. His left hand curled around a crumpled envelope. That was the real reason Jonah had felt so awful saying good-bye to his parents. Suddenly the shadows from the scrubby oaks and pines around the cabin seemed longer and more ominous.

Almost against his will, Jonah pulled the envelope out and turned it over in his hands. It was addressed "To the Parents of Jonah Lander." He swallowed hard.

He had only meant to have a quick look at the letter when it came in the mail three days ago. It hadn't even been sealed. Not all the way.

When his English teacher, Mr. Ritchie, had found the design for a motor scooter in Jonah's writing journal instead of his weekly assignment, Jonah had known he was in for some trouble. It had happened plenty of times before. Whenever he was supposed to be writing a story for English, his mind always wandered. Then he'd start sketching his machines instead. He couldn't help it.

Maybe it had been because Jonah had finally hit on a solution to the scooter design problem he'd been working on. Or it might have been that heady, reckless feeling of the last week of school. Either way, Jonah hadn't really thought through the consequences of not doing his last assignment for Mr. Ritchie.

Jonah stared at the outside of the envelope. He didn't have to take out the letter. He knew the contents by heart.

Dear Mr. and Ms. Lander:

At our last meeting, we agreed that I would contact you with any new concerns about Jonah's performance in English class. Although he did maintain a barely passing grade during the final marking period, Jonah did not turn in his final written assignment. On the report card to be mailed next week, he will receive an "Incomplete" in English.

In order for Jonah to move into eighth-grade English, he must complete the assignment. I will expect him to turn in a piece of fiction on any topic, of at least six double-spaced, typed pages, by August first. Then Jonah will attend summer school in early August for three follow-up sessions to edit his work. "Incomplete" is an option we use rarely, and only when we are certain that parents will support the student's efforts. If Jonah does not meet these requirements, he will have to be placed in the remedial English class next fall. Please call me at your earliest convenience to discuss.

Sincerely yours,
Edward Ritchie

Jonah's parents weren't going to support his writing efforts. They weren't going to call Mr. Ritchie "to discuss." They couldn't—they were on their way to Europe. Jonah was on his own. He blew out a long, defeated breath. What could he possibly make himself write about for six whole pages?

"Remedial English, here I come," Jonah said. He tried not to think about what his parents would say when they found out he hadn't passed English after all.

"What?" Jaye banged back out onto the porch, making him jump.

"Nothing." Jonah shoved the letter back into his pocket. He felt sick. How would he ever face his parents? Telling himself he hadn't wanted to ruin their trip didn't change a thing.

He had stolen the letter.

Chapter 2

Jaye shoved her bags into the little room she and Jonah were going to share. "I want to go swimming," she said for the thirty-seventh time.

Jonah ignored her and slid his duffel bag into a corner.

"Tell you what, Jayefish," Uncle Nate said, peeking into the room. "Let's go check out the old salt pond." He reached out and grabbed one of her braids. "Tug, you're it!"

Uncle Nate raced across the living room and out the front door of the cabin. He jumped off of the low, wooden deck. His long legs took him flying over bushes and brambles, and his springy mop of hair bounced up and down with each leap.

Jaye took off after him. "I'll get you, Uncle Nate!" she yelled.

Jonah followed them. He found Jaye standing at the edge of a small dock. Uncle Nate had disappeared.

"Where'd he go?" she demanded. "Uncle Nate?" Her voice rose into a squeak—excited, but with a hint of fear around the edges.

A large bush next to the dock shook.

"Yaaah!" Uncle Nate leaped out and grabbed Jaye.

She squealed as Uncle Nate hoisted her over his shoulder and ran for the end of the dock. "Wait! My clothes!"

"One..." Uncle Nate held Jaye out over the water.

"Jonah!" Jaye waved her arms at him. "Help!"

"Two..." Uncle Nate wound back in a swing. "Should I do it?" he called to Jonah.

Jaye kicked off her sneakers. She was laughing.

Jonah eyed the water uneasily. "Well—"

"Three!" Jaye cried.

Uncle Nate jumped off the dock with Jaye in his arms. He teetered, but stayed on his feet, raising a cloud of silt in the waist-deep water. He held her aloft another moment, then dropped her in with a splash.

She stood up sputtering and lunged for Uncle Nate.

"You said you wanted to go swimming," he teased. He dodged just out of her grasp.

Jaye shrieked with laughter. Jonah shook his head and smiled.

Maybe Uncle Nate could help me with my story, Jonah thought. He is a writer, after all. It might even be a relief to tell him about the letter. Jonah felt better already. His uncle would know what to do.

Jonah sat down on an overturned shell of a boat near the trees and watched his sister and his uncle chase each other around the shallows. After a while, Jaye paddled off on her own. Uncle Nate waded toward the shore. He stopped and lifted one foot out of the water, tipping something pale green and wriggling from his shoe.

Jonah sucked in a breath.

"Go home," Uncle Nate said. The slippery creature dropped into the water. He jerked his thumb over his shoulder at the pond and grinned at Jonah. "Pretty nice, huh?"

Jonah looked out at the salt pond. The expanse of blue-green water was more like a lake—or a bay, even—than what he'd imagined a pond to be. A few small sailboats angled in the evening breeze, and a windsurfer tipped his board, skimming the surface. Far off, an outboard motor droned. The sound reminded Jonah of the giant black bees that dive-bombed his head in the park back home. Funny to be way out here at the shore thinking about city bees. Right now he wished he didn't have to think about city anything. He took a deep breath. He had to tell Uncle Nate about the letter from Mr. Ritchie before he lost his nerve.

He decided to work his way into it. "Hey, Uncle Nate?" he said. "How do you get ideas for your stories?"

His uncle squelched out of the pond and sat down beside Jonah on the upturned hull. "My stories? I just look around, I guess. And I think about interesting things that've happened to me."

"When the kids in my school write stories, they're like, 'I got up in the morning. I went to school. I came home. The end.' Nothing really interesting ever happens to us."

"Untrue." Uncle Nate shook his head. "Interesting things always happen. You've just got to keep your eyes open. Or..." He glanced over at Jonah with a grin. "Or you can make stuff up. That's part of the fun. Take me, for instance—right now I'm writing a romance."

Gross, Jonah thought.

"Unfortunately, I'm not having one. A romance, I

mean." Uncle Nate gave a short laugh. "So I'm inventing the whole thing."

Uncle Nate's smile faded, and his bony shoulders sagged. He looked off into the distance. "It is hard work, though," he said slowly, almost as if he were talking to himself. "Takes concentration to write. No distractions."

No distractions. Something about those words made Jonah uneasy. What kind of distractions did he mean?

His uncle spoke again. "Selling the car bought me this one last, glorious summer to write." He sighed. "It's almost impossible, but I've got to try and finish my whole book this summer. Next summer I'll probably be working, not writing."

"But you're the manager of a ski resort. How can you work in the summer?"

"Well, they've added pools, waterslides, and whatnot. For now, someone else is managing the summer season, but I don't think I'll be able to afford to take next summer off to write. It looks like I'll have to rent out this place and run the water park instead."

Could this really be Uncle Nate talking? Jonah had never heard him sound so glum. Uncle Nate had a lot of writing to do, and that bad-news letter from Mr. Ritchie would be a distraction for sure. He couldn't tell Uncle Nate about it now.

Jonah rested his chin in his hands. His sister scooted along, belly in the water. He watched her grab for some kind of moving target under the surface. Jonah shuddered. Without wanting to, he remembered everything about his encounter with the Portuguese man-of-war.

They'd been on vacation in Florida, and Jonah had been swimming in the ocean. Bobbing along on the waves, the jellyfish had looked like a blue gum bubble someone had blown up and lost in the water. But gum bubbles didn't send you to the hospital in shock with a leg swollen to three times its normal size.

The pain of the sting had been fiery hot at first. Then Jonah's skin had turned to ice all over. He'd gasped for air, unable to catch his breath. He'd been dizzy and weak; his father had to carry him into the hospital like a baby. The last thing Jonah remembered before he passed out was throwing up all over the emergency room nurse.

"I'm afraid you just made it worse when you tried to rub the tentacles off," the doctor had told him later. "Thousands of stinging cells on these long strings under the water, and every one of them fired right into your leg." The doctor wiggled her fingers. "Sometimes bits of the tentacles are just loose in the water. You never even see them before they get you."

Even now, just thinking about it made Jonah's heart pound in his chest.

"Going in?" Uncle Nate asked him.

"No!" Jonah said, edging a bit nearer to the cabin. He couldn't swim in water like that. Not after that man-of-war sting. *You never even see them before they get you.* He looked away from the pond and tried to sound casual. "I mean, I'm a pool swimmer. I'm up to the first level of the lifesaving class at the Y."

"But you like the deep blue sea, right?" Uncle Nate cocked his head toward the strip of grassy dunes that separated the salt pond from the ocean.

Jonah glanced over just in time to see a small, muddy-looking flicker at the edge of the water. He shook his head. "Not really."

"Lakes?"

Jonah thought about that for a moment. "Nope."

"Hmmm. Didn't know that about you, Toolboy." Uncle Nate pushed to his feet and headed for the cabin. His shoes squished with each step.

"Uncle Nate?" Jonah called.

The squishing stopped.

"Where is the pool, anyway?"

Uncle Nate turned and gave Jonah an odd look. "The pool?"

"For the summer swim team. We're signed up, right? To go to practices, and be in meets against other town teams and stuff?"

Uncle Nate cleared his throat. "Couldn't sign Jaye up—she's a little too young. She's going to camp."

Jonah glanced over at Jaye in the water and rolled his eyes. Uh-oh. It had better be some kind of swim camp, or he'd be hearing about it, all right.

His uncle squished back to the boat hull and stood next to Jonah. "You see that beach across the way? The one with the pavilion and the rectangle of roped floats?"

"Is that the camp?"

"Well, ye-es." Uncle Nate shifted from side to side. His wet shoes made loud sucking noises.

There was more, Jonah figured. And it was going to be bad news.

"The campers swim in that roped-off area. And that's where the summer swim team practices, too. Lots of these

11

small towns around here have someplace like that—it's a kind of ponds and lakes division of the swim club, I guess."

Jonah stared across the pond at the floats. *That's where the summer swim team practices?*

He felt Uncle Nate's hand ruffle through his hair for the briefest moment. Then he heard his uncle slosh back toward the cabin. The screen door shut with a bang.

"Hey, Jonah! Look what I got!"

He dragged his gaze back to their edge of the pond. His sister was holding something up in the air. A something that had more waving legs than he wanted to know about.

Jonah stood up and put his hands in his pockets. The letter was still there.

Here's a good story, he thought.

"What I Did on My Summer Vacation"
I went to my uncle's cabin. I stayed out of the pond.
The End

It was going to need a little work.

CHAPTER 3

"Any girls on your swim team, or just boys?" Jaye's words hung somewhere near the low ceiling in their closet of a room in Uncle Nate's cabin. Jonah lay on his back and studied the grid of rusty springs on the underside of her bunk. He was trying not to think about it, but clearly his sister wasn't able to get the swim team off her waterlogged brain.

The mattress bowed toward Jonah's face with a twang that set his teeth on edge. The bunk bed's frame lurched. He screwed his eyes shut, certain he was about to be squashed like a waffle in a waffle iron. Nothing happened. When he opened his eyes, Jaye was peering at him. Her dark braids dangled over the side.

"Well?" she demanded.

"Well what?"

She swung her pillow at him. "Are there girls, or aren't there?"

"Who cares if there are girls on the swim team? I don't." Jonah ducked out of the lower bunk and slipped a pair of shorts on over his boxers. He heard the outdoor shower come on. Uncle Nate was awake. The water heater in the corner started to rattle and hiss like a subway train. Steam leaked from a loose fitting. Jonah dug in his bag for his toolbox. After tapping the rusty nut a few times to get it to turn, he tightened it with a wrench. The hissing stopped.

The room was so dim that Jonah wasn't even sure if the sun was up. He crossed to the window in a step and a half. Outside the dirty screen, patterns shifted between the trees. Bright flecks glinted off the surface of the salt pond. The morning air was damp and cool, and goose bumps rose on Jonah's arms.

"I know *you* don't care, Jonah, but *I* do."

Jonah rolled his eyes. Sometimes his sister had an uncanny way of reading other people's thoughts. But she was wrong about one thing. He did care about the swim team. Just not the same way she did.

The bunk bed screaked as Jaye turned away from him. "I should be on the team, not you." She kicked the wall, hard. "I'm the top backstroker at the Y. Top in butterfly, too, when Allen Pinkwater's not there."

Jonah leaned against the top bunk. "Look, Jaye," he said to her back. "What can I do? Uncle Nate says you have to be twelve for this team."

"But they signed me up for *arts and crafts camp!*"

The way she shuddered out the words, it sounded more like walking-on-a-bed-of-nails camp, or liver-and-onions camp.

"Uncle Nate told you that you'd get to go swimming," Jonah said. "I mean, come on, Jaye, the camp's at the town beach."

"I have to *train* this summer, Jonah," Jaye wailed, "not

make arts and crafts. If I don't, May Lin will get faster than me. She's going to sleep-away swim camp for a whole week!"

Jonah leaned his forehead on his hands and closed his eyes. Sleeping away hadn't worked out that well for him so far. The snapping branches, high-pitched cheeps, and sudden trills had kept him on high alert all night. He couldn't figure out how Jaye had fallen right to sleep. He'd lain in the bunk below her thinking wistfully of his own room, with the ebb and flow of traffic out his window and the comfortable hum of the air conditioner.

Jaye flopped over to face him. "Well, I've decided. I'm not going to any dumb arts and crafts camp. I can stay right here and swim with Uncle Nate all day."

Jonah looked up. "You can't do that, Jaye. He's going to be busy writing his book, and he wants us to have something to do. Problem is, it's kind of the middle of nowhere here. Not like the city, you know?" He forced himself to say it. "There aren't a whole lot of choices."

The bad feeling that had been niggling at Jonah in the night returned. Nothing was turning out the way he'd hoped. Had Uncle Nate had a choice about all of this? Did he even want them here? Jonah tried to remember their faces—his parents' and Uncle Nate's—when they'd said good-bye the afternoon before. He wished he'd paid closer attention. But he'd been thinking about the letter and not much else.

He flicked a guilty glance at his jeans lying on the floor. A tiny triangle of white envelope was visible at the edge of the pocket. Too late, he felt Jaye watching his face.

He lunged, but she had already leaped off of the bunk.

His sister got there first. She yanked the envelope out of the jeans and waved it in the air.

"Give it!" Jonah yelled. He grabbed for the letter, but she held her arm high over her head. They stood almost eye to eye. Why did she have to be so tall for a ten-year-old girl, with those long swimmer arms? Why was he, as his mother had charitably told him, still waiting for his thirteen-year-old "growth spurt"?

Jonah grabbed both of Jaye's arms and forced them down to her sides, plucking the envelope from her fingers. He crumpled it into a ball and stuffed it into his shorts pocket.

Jaye's lower lip quivered. She rubbed her arms. "I saw the writing. That letter was for Mom and Dad. From your school. You're in trouble, aren't you, Jonah?"

The noise from the shower outside stopped. Uncle Nate would be coming in soon.

"Not really," Jonah lied. "It's just this story I forgot to finish for my English teacher. No big deal."

"So Mom and Dad know about it, then?"

Jonah wished she would drop the subject. Every lie he told seemed to lead him into another. "Uh, sure they do."

"Did they tell Uncle Nate?"

They heard the screen door bang.

"No," Jonah lowered his voice. "Uncle Nate has a lot on his mind. They didn't want to bother him. I'm going to finish it myself and mail it to school. Don't worry about it."

"Hey, sleepyheads!" Uncle Nate called.

"You're not going to bother Uncle Nate with this, right?" Jonah whispered.

She turned her back to him and folded her arms. "Jonah's coming out, Uncle Nate," she said in a loud voice. "I'm going to get dressed now."

Did Jaye believe him about the letter? Jonah wasn't sure. Stealing the letter had gotten him to Uncle Nate's, but now that he was here, things weren't going as well as he'd hoped. He knelt down and pulled a T-shirt from his bag. Jonah glanced at Jaye. Her back was still turned.

"I'm waiting," she said.

"I'm just grabbing a shirt," Jonah told her. Satisfied that she wasn't watching, he slipped the letter out of his pocket and hid it under his toolbox.

"Well?" she demanded without turning around. "Aren't you done yet?"

CHAPTER 4

Jonah ducked around the curtain hanging across the doorway into the cabin's main room. Sun shimmered through the plate glass window, making him squint. A salty breeze brought the cries of gulls from beyond the barrier beach.

"Hey there." Uncle Nate was rubbing his hair with a towel. "Pull up a seat."

Jonah slid onto a high stool with his back to the sun. When he saw what was on the kitchen counter, his mouth dropped open. Every sugary cereal his mother had ever refused to buy was lined up next to a stack of giant soup bowls.

Jaye peeked out from behind the curtain. Jonah watched her warily, wondering if she was still thinking about the letter. He didn't have to worry. The second she saw the row of cereals on the counter, her eyes grew big and round.

"Wow!" She slid across the painted wood floor in her socks and leaped onto the stool next to Jonah's. It spun in a circle.

Uncle Nate reached over and gave her an extra spin.

"Wow? Wow, you say?" He spun her again. "Does that mean, 'Wow, Uncle Nate's the best'? or 'Wow, Uncle Nate's really crazy'?" He sent the stool in another circle.

"The crazy best!" Jaye gasped. "The crazy best!"

"Crazy best, eh? Very diplomatic, Jayefish. You sure you're only ten?" Uncle Nate teased. "Well, since breakfast's such a hit, let's see if I can go two for two. I got you guys these." He handed them each a spiral notebook. "They're journals." He reached across the counter and opened Jonah's. "See? Clean, empty pages waiting for you like..." Uncle Nate swept his hand toward the salt pond. "...like uncharted waters. Just waiting for your summer story."

Jonah felt his face turn as white as the pages. Did Uncle Nate already know about the letter? He shot a glance at Jaye. She was leafing through her journal.

"This is great, Uncle Nate!" she exclaimed.

"You don't have to *write* if you don't want to, Jonah. Sheesh!" Uncle Nate shook his head. "What a face! You can draw things, too." He tossed a big pack of colored pencils on the counter. "Pictures of shells you find, birds, fish." He leaned toward Jonah. "Socket wrenches..."

Jonah let his breath out in a whoosh. This whole journal thing seemed to be just a coincidence—an unfortunate, panic-inducing coincidence. He gave his uncle a weak smile and flipped through the pages of the notebook.

"That's better," his uncle said. "But tsk, tsk! How could you go all glum when your uncle, the *writer*, mentions the word 'story'? You'd think writing stories was a bad thing."

Jonah shot a glance at Jaye. She'd already poured a bowl of cereal and was busy shoveling it into her mouth.

"No, it's great, Uncle Nate," he said. "Really, thanks."

"Mm going to wri' a story *and* draw picthures," Jaye said, sending a spray of chocolate cereal onto the counter.

"Maybe you should start with something more basic," Jonah told her. "Like chewing and swallowing."

She swung her leg at him under the counter and missed. Her stool spun around again.

"Well, guys, speaking of stories..." Uncle Nate walked over to a small table and picked up his writing notebook. "Sorry about this, but I have to get to work. You two make yourselves at home. There are tons of books." He waved his hand at the shelves all around the room. "And that cabinet is full of games. There are some dip nets and buckets down by the dock." His words came out in a rush, like he'd practiced them. "I'm going to write here in the mornings. I'll work in my room most of the time. I probably won't come up for air much, but I'm here if you need me."

Jonah frowned at the floor. So that was how it was going to be—Uncle Nate working all morning, and the two of them gone every afternoon? Even with all his worries, Jonah had figured that hanging out with his uncle was the one thing he could count on. It was something he had taken for granted. Now he'd not only have to swim in a creepy-crawly pond every afternoon, but he'd also be stuck watching Jaye in the mornings. And she always wanted to do the same thing.

"But when will you come swimming with me?" Jaye whined.

"We'll have weekends...and every evening," Uncle Nate said. "It's the best time here, anyway." He walked to the big window and shaded his eyes. He made a stick figure of a silhouette against the sunny window, his ripped cotton sweater bagging at the elbows. "Remember last night, how the sun set over there?" He pointed toward the cove. "The air gets all purple and dusty blue, and the water's soft and so warm. Everything quiets down like the tender, slow part of a symphony. It makes your heart want to burst." He turned and hugged his notebook to his chest. "Like when you're falling in love."

Jonah gave him a look.

"I know, I know!" Uncle Nate hit himself over the head with the notebook. "This story's made me a little mushy around the edges. I'll tell you one thing, though. Those Victorians knew about love, all right." He clasped his notebook over his heart. "They could appreciate the littlest things: the curve of a cheek, moonlit gardens, a lingering glance." He batted his eyes at Jaye and she giggled. "It was so, so—"

"So romantic," Jaye swooned.

"So nauseating," Jonah muttered.

Uncle Nate opened the door to his bedroom. "Okeydokey then, guys. Help yourselves to the fridge. By the way, Toolboy, I picked up two extra bikes at a yard sale," he said. "They're leaning on the side of the cabin if you want to take a look. They're for you and Jaye to ride to swim team and camp after lunch."

Jaye poked Jonah in the ribs with her sharp elbow. It hurt. As if he needed any other painful reminders about the swim team.

Their uncle didn't seem to notice. "See you later," he said.

As soon as the bedroom door shut, Jaye turned to Jonah. "Let's go swimming."

"Jaye—"

Uncle Nate opened his door again and poked his head out.

"One more thing," he said with an apologetic look. "I know you're both swimmers, but your parents made me promise that you wouldn't go in the water without an adult on the premises."

"So we can go as long as you're here?" Jaye said.

"Not here," Uncle Nate said, pointing at his bedroom. "More like here." He gestured toward the deck and the dock beyond.

"But—"

"That's okay." Jonah cut her off. He smiled at his uncle. "We'll stay out of the water. No problem."

"Okeydokey then." Uncle Nate nodded. He pulled his head back into his room and shut the door.

Jonah rubbed his side. "Why'd you poke me like that?" he said to Jaye in a low voice. "I can't do anything about the swim team."

Jaye shrugged.

"And oh, don't forget—you don't need to bother Uncle Nate about that letter." Jonah tried to sound like it was nothing important.

"Why are you so worried about it, anyway?" Jaye said, looking at him closely.

"I'm not worried about it," Jonah insisted. "I just don't want you to worry about it, either."

"Well, I won't worry about it if you get me on the swim team."

Jonah turned slowly. Jaye looked a little scared, but her pointy jaw was firm.

"But Jaye—"

"That's the deal." She took her new journal, spun on her heel, and pushed through the curtain to their room.

Jonah heard the springs on the bunk bed squeak. Stealing, lying, now blackmail. What else would this summer bring him? He shook his head and went out the back screen door.

Jonah found the bikes leaning against the outside wall of the cabin. They were low slung, with fat tires and long, low saddles. Kind of old-fashioned, he thought. They'd probably do pretty well on the sandy roads that led to the town beach. Jonah grabbed one of the bikes by its V-shaped handlebars and walked it toward the dirt driveway. The chain ground along on its sprockets for a few turns, then fell off. He leaned the bike against a tree and went to get his toolbox.

* * *

Three hours later Jonah picked up his sweatshirt from the tree stump where he had tossed it and wiped his face. Done, he thought with satisfaction. Both bikes were now in good working order. He slumped to the ground with his back against the outside wall of the cabin. The sun was almost directly overhead. Sounds of shouts and splashes reached his ears from across the pond. Jonah checked his watch and groaned. How had it gotten so late already?

The screen door creaked open. Uncle Nate came out, with Jaye following him. It banged shut behind them.

"Since you guys will be leaving soon, I'm going to pedal over to the library in Gray Harbor," Uncle Nate said. "My novel is set in Victorian times, so I have some historical research to finish. Got to study up on my waistcoats and corsets, you know." He smiled and squashed his hair under an old, round helmet. "Both of you brought these, right?" He knocked on his head.

"Right," Jaye said. She eyed Uncle Nate's scuffed white dome. "But ours are a little, uh, different shape."

"Well, funny-shaped ones will probably work, too."

Jonah grinned.

Uncle Nate straddled his bicycle, one foot ready to pedal and one on the ground. "If you stay on this road, no turns, you can ride almost all the way around the pond. The road doesn't go to the breachway—that's where the pond connects to the Sound. But that area's off limits for you, anyway. I'm going this way." He turned his bike to the right. "If you go that way," Uncle Nate said, pointing left, "you'll pass the general store, the park, and then you'll come to the town beach and pavilion. Camp and practice both start at one o'clock, so you'll need to leave in a few minutes." He scooted his bike out to the road. "Well, I guess I'm off, then." His helmet slid forward onto the bridge of his nose and he pushed it up. "Have a great day, you two!"

They watched him wobble away down the sandy road. His knees stuck out at sharp angles on either side of the bicycle. He went around a curve and was out of sight.

"We'd better go, too," Jaye said. "You'll never believe what Uncle Nate made us for lunch. Peanut butter and fluff sandwiches! I had mine already, but you can eat yours on the way. While you think of your plan to get me on the swim team."

Peanut butter and fluff on a bike. Great, Jonah thought. Maybe choking to death would keep him out of the pond. But it wouldn't get Jaye on this so-called swim team for kids twelve and over. How was he going to do that?

CHAPTER 5

When Jonah and Jaye arrived at the town beach and pavilion, they saw a burly man lecturing a line of kids down near the water. He wore a big silver whistle around his neck and held a clipboard in front of his face. He didn't look up.

This just gets better and better, Jonah thought. He took off his helmet and parked his bike. We're going swimming in a creepy-crawly pond with a coach who never even looks in the water. Anything could be lurking under the surface—things that bite, things that sting—

A poke in his side made Jonah jump.

"See?" Jaye whispered. "There *are* girls on the team."

The coach squinted at the clipboard.

"Barrows!" he barked.

"Here," a large boy answered.

Jonah looked at the twenty or so kids standing on the beach. They weren't all big like that Barrows kid. Jaye was as tall as some of the smaller ones. Maybe she could pass for twelve. But where did that leave him? He looked out at the roped-off area in time to see a good-sized fish launch itself out of the water. As the fish splashed back in, a whole school of silvery somethings streaked away underneath the surface in a flurry. Jonah took a step back.

"Why are you making that face?" Jaye whispered. "Are you afraid of the coach?"

"No. Are you sure you want to swim here?"

"Of course. Just ask him if I can join, too."

"Be quiet and let me think a minute," Jonah hissed. He edged a little closer, stopping in the shadow of the line of trees at the edge of the sand.

"Dransky!" the coach shouted.

"Here." A tall, thin girl raised her hand. The coach never lifted his eyes from the clipboard.

"Evanston!"

"Here," answered a boy standing near the back of the group.

"Fullman!"

"Here," squeaked a girl with short blond hair.

The coach didn't seem to have heard her. "L. Fullman!" he shouted again.

"Here," the blond girl squeaked again.

The coach continued down his list, last names only.

"Higgins!"

A freckle-faced boy ran past Jonah, kicking sand, and fell in at the end of the line.

"R. Higgins!"

"Here," the boy huffed, holding his sides.

Last names, Jonah thought. Last names and sometimes initials. That was it! He grabbed Jaye and pulled her over behind the trees, out of earshot of the kids and counselors at the pavilion. "You're J. Lander," he said, shaking her by the shoulders. "Get it?"

His sister looked at him as if he had gone completely mad. "What are you talking about? I've been Jaye Lander since the day I was born. Where've you been?" She shimmied out of his grasp.

"No, I mean *J*. The initial *J*. This coach doesn't even care if you're a boy or a girl. You're going to be me!" Jonah was practically hopping up and down. "You see the way he calls out the names? When he gets to my name on the list, he'll just say 'Lander.' Worst case, he'll say 'J. Lander.'"

Jaye's dark eyebrows knitted together. "But—"

Jonah interrupted her. "You just say 'here,'" he hurried on. "Nice and loud, too. If anyone says anything to you about you being Jonah, tell them to call you Jaye. They'll think you mean the letter *J*. Like it's a nickname initial, see?"

"B-but Jonah," Jaye stammered, clutching at his arm. "Wait! I don't know anyone here. I thought we were going to be on the team together. Why don't you—"

Jonah took her hand and led her over to the line of kids.

"Kohl!" the coach yelled out.

"Here," a girl in a pink bathing suit said. She was just the same size as Jaye.

"I think I'm—you're going to be next," Jonah said under his breath to Jaye. "Do you want to be on the team, or don't you?" He backed out of the line.

"Lander!" the coach called.

Jonah watched Jaye out of the corner of his eye. She just stood there. She didn't say a word. Why didn't she answer "here"? One little word, and they'd both be home free.

"J. Lander!"

Please, Jonah prayed.

"Is Lander here, or not?" the coached barked.

She wasn't going to do it. Jonah's heart sank. He moved closer to the line. He was going to have to be on the team. He was going to have to get in that pond.

"Here," he mumbled. He could barely get the word out.

"What?" the coach shouted.

"HERE!"

Jonah jerked his head around to look at his sister. Her face was a deep crimson. "I'm here," she said again, loud and clear.

CHAPTER 6

When Jonah was out of sight of the pavilion, he let out a yell. He yanked up on his bike handlebars and spun in a circle on the rear tire. It felt so good that he did it again and again until he was dizzy and tipped over into the hot sand at the side of the road. He rolled onto his back and rested his head on his hands.

The arts and crafts counselor had seemed genuinely disappointed that Jaye wouldn't be joining her group. She had assured Jonah that a refund would be sent to his parents' address in the city. And there it would sit, in the growing pile at the post office, until they returned at the end of July.

Perfect, Jonah thought.

He stood up, brushed the sand off, and righted his bike. Saluting in the direction he had come, he called out, "Good-bye, creature-infested salt pond!" His voice disappeared down the empty road.

It was too hot to ride around. Jonah headed back along the road toward the cabin. He could wait for Uncle Nate to get back from the library. Maybe he'd take Jonah climbing on the dunes. It would be great to goof around, just the two of them.

Jonah stopped short and stood straddling his bike.

I've got to finish my book, Uncle Nate had said.

Uncle Nate wasn't going to goof around. Jonah was supposed to be busy with the swim team in the afternoons so Uncle Nate could work. *No distractions.*

A horn blared. Jonah scooted over as an old red truck with a double cab rumbled by.

"Side of the road, airhead!" The driver jerked his thumb out the open window.

Jonah turned his back to the truck and its kicked-up dust. He scowled.

What would Uncle Nate say when he found out that Jonah wasn't on the swim team? He might be angry. Or worse, disappointed. Jonah couldn't bear that. He sat back on the bike seat and laced his fingers on top of his head. If he couldn't go back to the cabin, where could he go?

He followed the road along the edge of the pond until it bowed around the empty brown field of the park. Jonah set his bike in the rack and sat down on an old swing. The long chains made sounds like the seagulls he had heard earlier that morning.

Jonah kicked at the sand with the toe of his sneaker. Back home in the city, his park had a basketball court, a handball court, and a ramp for skateboard tricks. Last time Uncle Nate had come for a visit, he'd whipped thirty or so kids into a crazy tag free-for-all through the park's giant climbing maze.

Jonah scooped up a stone and threw it as far as he could. He squinted after it. At the other end of the field, the surface of the salt pond glared in the sun. A motorboat passed, leaving a thin white trail. Far to the right, in front of the pavilion, Jonah saw the swim team bobbing in the water for warm-ups. He could just make out Jaye's dark braids. They flapped up and down, up and down, right in time with the rest of the team. That ought to keep her happy for the next four hours, he thought.

He left the swings and went to climb the spindly jungle gym. It shook under his weight, and the hot metal burned his palms. Giving up on the park, Jonah trudged back to his bike. He was getting very thirsty.

A few hundred yards past the park, the road curved away from the salt pond. Trees were thicker here—pines and leafy shrubs laced together. If he kept riding along the road, Jonah knew that he would eventually get back to the cabin. He'd have to turn around again before he got too close. Not exactly a brilliant plan for the afternoon.

As Jonah zigzagged his bike along the road, a small sign in the shape of a boat caught his eye. Faint sounds of music and sporadic hammering drifted through the trees. He turned off the road and followed an arrow down a wide sandy lane.

The woods gave way to a view of a narrow cove. When he saw the soda machine leaning against a ramshackle building, Jonah almost cheered out loud. He leaned his bike against the side of the building and pulled a handful of change from his pocket.

Half of the quarters he deposited came back to him, along with a Coke in an old-fashioned glass bottle. Scratchy radio tunes drifted from the open door of the store. Jonah didn't go in. He drained his soda in one long series of gulps, tossed the empty bottle into a crate, and bought another.

The store was perched at the edge of a labyrinth of floating aluminum docks. A couple of trucks were parked on the hard-packed sand. Boats were everywhere—tied to the docks, moored out in the water, hauled out on trailers, or belly-up on the grass. It reminded Jonah of the marina in Florida where they'd rented a boat—before he'd gotten stung by the Portuguese man-of-war. His father had taken the cover off the small outboard motor to show Jonah the inside and had taught him how to start it. He'd even let him drive the boat a few times. That had been the best part of the vacation.

Jonah stepped down onto one of the long docks with a reverberating clang. A guy was working on a big fishing boat at the far end. He didn't look up. Between the slats, Jonah could see schools of drab fish darting in the mucky shallows. He turned and stepped carefully back onto dry land. Better to look around at the trailered boats, he decided.

He came upon a sleek black motorboat tipped on its side. It had a ragged hole in its hull. Tucked in the shade underneath it were several large metal cans, some paper buckets and brushes, and a heap of white folded cloth. The boat's big outboard motor sat on a wooden stand. The motor's cover lay in the grass, the number 185 in gleaming, slanted letters on its side. One hundred and eighty-five horsepower—that was a big motor! Would the head of that motor look the same inside as the smaller one he'd seen in Florida? Jonah glanced over his shoulder. No one was around.

He sidled up to the motor and looked inside. There were six spark plugs. He wondered if they came out the same way the ones in his family's station wagon did. He looked around again, then reached in and pulled off the spark plugs' rubber boots. A spark plug wrench lay on the ground nearby. He took the rusty white plugs out one by one, examining the gaps.

This thing needs some work, he thought, dropping the spark plugs into an empty paint bucket. The motor had six carburetors, linked together in three sets of two. Jonah stuck his fingers in and flapped the butterfly valves up and down. They needed cleaning, he thought. Too bad he didn't have a spray can of light machine oil handy.

With his dirty fingers, Jonah pulled at a tiny fuse in a little black fuse holder. Its filaments looked worn. Why would that be, he wondered? He checked the wires around the fuse holder. Were they tight? He had trouble getting a grip on the wires as he pulled on them to check each connection. Sweat beaded on his forehead and trickled down his back. Just one more wire, he thought.

Pop! The last wire snapped. Jonah pulled his hand out of the motor and stepped back. Just then, someone grabbed the back of his shirt.

"What the hell do you think you're doin'?" an angry voice snarled in his ear.

CHAPTER 7

I just asked what the hell you're doin'!" Jonah twisted around. He found himself looking into a face with more lines than the city subway map.

"Whatsa matter? Can't talk?" The old man chomped on a cigar, his white-bristled chin going up and down. He shook Jonah by his shirt. "Who are you, anyway?"

Jonah tried to free himself, but the hand on his shirt was like a clamp. I don't have to tell this guy anything, he thought. He stopped struggling and pulled himself up straight.

"Who are *you*?" he challenged.

The old man stared. The cigar stopped moving. He let go of Jonah's shirt and bent double. His stocky shoulders heaved, and he made choking sounds.

What was happening here? Jonah's mind cast around in a panic for the CPR rules he'd learned in lifesaving class. Was it one breath and five chest compressions? Or five breaths and one chest compression?

Abruptly the old man stood up. He pulled the knitted watch cap off of his coarse white hair and wiped his eyes with it.

That had all been some weird kind of laugh, Jonah realized. But the fun seemed to be over now. The man glared at Jonah, scratching his chest through his grease-stained shirt.

"Who am *I?*" he growled. "Who am *I? Who do you think?*" He jerked his head toward the building.

Jonah made out the words "Bert's General Store and Marina" in faded lettering across the side wall. Obviously this was Bert.

"This here's my place. I own it. I'm on top of everything that goes on around here, see?" Bert held his cigar stub between his thumb and forefinger, turned his face away, and *zzzt!* sent a brown stream of spit toward the bushes. "Don't bother tellin' me who *you* are."

Jonah stopped breathing.

Bert leaned in close. "I already know," he said. His bushy eyebrows bristled.

Jonah's heart pounded. If this guy did know, he'd go straight to Uncle Nate. Then the whole deal to switch with Jaye on the swim team would be down the tubes.

"Wait—"

"I know three things about you, an' that's all I need," Bert growled. He held up a stubby finger. "One, you're a summer kid."

Jonah felt his face go red.

"Two..." Bert pointed a second finger at the wire in Jonah's hand. "You just cost me a pile of money by wreckin' the power pack in that motor."

Jonah stared at the piece of torn wire. "I-I didn't mean to break it," he stammered. "I can fix—"

"An' three," the old man said, ignoring him, "if you don't have a big wad of cash on you, you're going to have to find some other way to pay for the damage."

"But I don't—"

Bert interrupted again. "Well, since you don't have the money—and since you don't have anything better to do than mess with my stuff—looks like you're gonna have to work to make it right."

Questions raced around in Jonah's brain. Did this mean that Bert didn't really know who Jonah was? And what did he mean about working? Jonah had no idea what to say next.

"I want to make it right," he told Bert. "I do. But what—?"

The old man turned and headed off for the store.

Jonah stared after him. He looked at the wire in his hand. Work to make it right? Was Jonah supposed to fix that big motor right now? He glanced around the boat-yard. The guy at the far end of the dock jumped into the water with a loud splash. Jonah gulped. There were defi-nitely worse places he could be than a marina, he thought, eyeing the pond. He turned toward the ski boat and its 185 horsepower motor.

"Hey, summer kid," Bert snarled over his shoulder. "I said work. And it starts now. Let's go."

* * *

"When you finish with the crates, clean that up." Bert flicked his cigar at the utility sink next to the back door and went inside the store.

Jonah looked at the stack of greasy pots and pans in the outdoor sink, wreckage from Bert's short-order counter. He gave the last crate an angry kick. It crashed into the neat pile of twenty-odd crates he had already pulled apart, spilling wooden slats into a jumble on the ground.

The tinny radio noise stopped. He shot a look at the back door, half-expecting the old man to come out and yell at him. Instead, music and voices that sounded like a TV show drifted through the back door of the general store.

Jonah restacked the slats into a pile. He broke up the last crate and tied the slats into bundles with twine. He hauled the bundles, one after the other, to Bert's rusty white pickup and heaved them into the back. The trays of soda bottles he had rinsed with the hose were stacked next to the soda machine, already dry in the blazing afternoon sun. Jonah looked longingly at the full bottles he could see through the vending machine's glass front. But the old machine didn't give change for a dollar, and he wasn't about to go into the store to ask Bert for anything. He walked around back, squirted soap into the sink, and let it fill.

Up to his elbows in the sudsy water, Jonah worked his way through the dishes. That old guy is never letting me near the motor, he thought. I was crazy to think he'd ever let me touch it, let alone fix it myself. Jonah ground away at a blackened pan, scraping with a metal spatula until his arms ached. The front of his shirt was soaked. He straightened and stretched his back. There was no one in the boatyard now, and no movement in or on the water of the narrow inlet. The small strip of barrier beach visible far across the salt pond gleamed a blinding white.

Jonah filled a clean glass from the drying rack with cold water. He poured it over his head and shook, sending droplets in an arc like a wet dog. He refilled the glass and closed his eyes for a long drink.

"I oughta make you wash every one of 'em again."

Jonah dropped the glass in the dirty water with a splash.

"What do you think you're doin', shakin' water all over the clean glasses like that?" Bert held his cigar out and spat. "Wash that glass an' the rest out good. Come inside when you're done." He stepped back inside the store and let the door bang behind him.

Jonah leaned his elbows on the edge of the sink and rested his chin on his hands.

What was he doing here? How had his summer with Uncle Nate turned into this?

He looked down into the sink. What was it that Uncle Nate had said? *Interesting things always happen, if you're really looking for them.* He let out a quiet laugh and fished around in the soapy water. He extracted an egg-encrusted fork, its tines bent at crazy angles.

Yup, you've got to really look, Jonah thought. One thrill after another.

"What I Did on My Summer Vacation"
I went to my uncle's cabin.
I washed greasy dishes.
The End

39

Maybe I shouldn't have been so quick to give up my spot on the swim team, Jonah mused, examining the fork. Having a pond creature eat my toe off might have gotten me one page closer to passing English.

Jonah looked out again at the glittering pond for a moment, considering. No, no way. He shook his head and reached back into the murky gray sink water.

CHAPTER 8

Jonah wiped his hands on his pants and stepped in through the back door of the general store. After the glaring sunshine outside, he couldn't see anything for a minute.

"Here." It was Bert's voice.

A cellophane bag hit Jonah on the nose and skittered away on the floor. There was a burst of laughter.

"Same airhead look he had when I almost ran him down on his bike!"

"You got yourself a real live wire there, Bert!"

Another group laugh at Jonah's expense.

He ducked down behind the short-order griddle to retrieve the bag of chips. The two men sitting at the other end of the counter with Bert looked like a forty-something and a teenaged version of the same person. Bert chomped his cigar. The older man smirked at Jonah and the younger guy stared, chewing his gum with a snapping sound. Jonah busied himself opening the chips. His stomach rumbled and he was glad for the TV chatter and the whir of the large fan.

"Done out there?" Bert growled.

Jonah nodded.

"You still owe me. You set me back weeks on that motor by breakin' that power pack. Be back tomorrow."

The others chuckled. Jonah felt his face grow hot. "If I set you back so much," he said to Bert, "how come you weren't out there working on the motor?"

"Oh ho! Didja hear that, Len?" The older man bumped the younger one with his shoulder and guffawed.

"Yeah, how come you weren't out there working, Bert?" The younger guy laughed. He blew a round, pink bubble and sucked it back with a pop.

"Hey, Al—hey, Lenny—how about shuttin' up?" Bert dismissed the two with a wave of his cigar. "For fishermen, you two keep up pretty good on the soaps." He jerked his chin toward the small TV playing behind him.

"C'mon, Bert. We were out early, like every day. Fish ain't runnin' now," Al said.

"Me, I'm waitin' on a part," Bert said, glowering at Lenny. "Hey, you." The old man poked his cigar toward Jonah. "What's your name?"

"Jonah."

"Yeah, well, one easy day's work won't do it, kid. You're here tomorrow. The next day, too. Or don't you have the stickin' power?"

Jonah flung the bag of chips into the trash and slammed out of the store. He grabbed his bike. *One easy day's work!* Bert could take his sticking power and stick it himself. Standing on the pedals, Jonah forced the bike through the sand, his front tire wobbling.

Jonah heard laughter. "And stay out of the road, airhead!" a voice called after him.

He pedaled right down the middle of the road all the way back to the town beach. Jaye was waiting for him by the bike rack.

"Where *were* you?" she asked. She pulled her bike out and turned it around, climbing on. "I've been all done for a long time."

Jonah checked his watch. "It's just five after five, Jaye."

"Well, I want to get back. I can't wait to tell Uncle Nate about the swim team!"

Jonah looked at his sister sharply. "No! You can't tell him, Jaye."

"Why not?" She planted her feet on the ground. "I can tell him if I want."

"What if Uncle Nate says you can't do it because you're not twelve? Anyway, I don't want him to worry about me *not* being on the team," Jonah said.

"What do you mean? What did you tell him when he got back from the library?"

"I didn't go back to the cabin." Jonah started riding down the road.

Jaye pedaled hard to catch up. "Not at all? You just wandered around by yourself?"

"Well, I—"

"We're never allowed to do that. I'm telling!"

"No, Jaye! I know we don't hang around alone at home. But the rules are a little different here."

Jaye pedaled ahead. She wasn't buying.

"I wasn't hanging around by myself, anyway." Jonah hurried to catch her. "I got a job."

"You did not! A job? Where?" Jaye puffed.

"At the general store. I'm working at the general store."

Jaye stopped. She put her feet on the ground and turned to face him. "Prove it," she said. "Take me there."

He wasn't about to go back to that store. And Uncle Nate was waiting for them to get home. They couldn't be late on their very first day.

"I'll take you tomorrow, on the way to the swim team," Jonah stalled. He'd have to think of a way to put her off the next day.

"Okay," Jaye said. "But you'd better be telling *me* the truth about it." She got back on her bike and rode toward the cabin.

Jonah had to work for Bert. He didn't have anything else to do, anyway. But it wasn't a job. Not really. Not like he wanted Jaye to believe.

If it weren't for the writing part, I'd make a pretty good storyteller, Jonah thought with a frown. But there was nothing good about the feeling in the pit of his stomach as he watched one lie grow into another and another.

* * *

After dinner that night, Jonah sat on the upturned boat hull watching Jaye splash around in the water with Uncle Nate. Four hours of swim team and she still hadn't had enough. Jonah shook his head. She had even blabbed about swimming through bites of burger at dinner. Luckily Uncle Nate had thought she was talking about swim time at the arts and crafts camp. Jonah needn't have worried. Even if he had wanted to tell his uncle about his day, he never would have had the chance.

Uncle Nate came out of the water and sat down next to Jonah. "So, how about you? You managed okay today?"

"Y-yeah," Jonah said slowly. He *had* managed okay, sort of. He ran his hands along the boat hull, trying not to think too hard about what Uncle Nate was really asking. His fingers found a hole in the boat, and he picked at it absently. He felt his uncle's eyes on him, and he looked down at what his fingers were doing.

The sun was setting behind the cove, the evening air soft and cool. His face felt warmer than it should. "What happened to this boat?" Jonah asked.

"Huh?" Uncle Nate looked down at the hole. "You know, I'm not really sure what's up with this thing." He patted the skiff. "It belonged to a friend of mine who moved to California. He used it here a few times. I think he even had a motor for it, but that's gone now."

Uncle Nate stood up and walked around the skiff. He bent and grabbed the gunwale. Jonah caught the other side and together they righted her.

"The rest of this looks pretty good," Uncle Nate said. He looked at Jonah. "Are you interested in boats?"

"We rented one last year. I got to take the wheel. It was pretty cool."

"Think you can fix this one?"

Jonah looked at the gash in the fiberglass hull. He'd seen lots of cans and jars of repair materials near the black ski boat at Bert's marina. That stuff was probably expensive. Jonah didn't have the slightest idea how to use any of it, anyway.

"I saw one getting fixed," Jonah said, adding, "once."

Uncle Nate picked up his towel and snapped it at the hole. "You fix it, you bought it, Toolboy," he said. He chuckled at his own joke all the way up to the cabin.

Jonah climbed into the boat and sat on the molded seat in the stern. He looked out over the pond, remembering the boat ride in Florida. The evening breeze riffled his hair. This boat would definitely need a motor, he thought.

Chapter 9

Jonah watched Jaye stand up to pedal over a small rise in the pond road. He couldn't figure out why she hadn't bugged him about checking out his "job" at the general store on their way to swim team. And all morning, while they'd cleaned up the cabin, she had been uncharacteristically quiet. She hadn't said much at all to Uncle Nate before he went into his room to write.

The chores had been Jonah's idea. He'd thought it would feel like he was keeping up his end of things somehow. Jaye hadn't seemed to mind it. The cabin was so small, their work had seemed a little like playing house. They had straightened the small living room, stacking library books and magazines on the rickety coffee table. Then they'd swept the floor and wiped up in the kitchen. But no amount of cleaning in the morning had wiped away the fact that Uncle Nate believed Jonah would be on the swim team in the afternoon.

Jaye rode on ahead. Maybe she was too busy worrying about her butterfly stroke to remember about the marina. That would be good, Jonah thought. The last thing he needed was for Jaye to hear Bert grouse about him breaking the motor, and about Jonah owing only two days' work.

Jaye didn't really know how much trouble Jonah was in at school. And maybe she'd believed him when he'd told her that their parents already knew about the letter. He was probably safe on that front. But he knew it was asking a lot of his little sister to keep the swim team switch a secret. It could easily slip out, especially if she was curious about what he was doing the rest of the afternoons. Jonah chewed on the inside of his cheek and pedaled harder.

His sister disappeared around a bend in the road. The turnoff to the store and marina was coming soon. He sped up even more. He wanted to make sure she'd passed Bert's access road.

When he came around the bend, he didn't see Jaye on the pond road at all. How had she ridden so far ahead? What if Al's red pickup suddenly roared around a turn? Jonah was angry at himself for not keeping a better eye on his sister. He sped past the thick stand of trees flanking the access road to the general store.

"Looking for someone?"

Jonah swung his handlebars sideways and his bike slid out from under him. One of the pedals caught him in the back of the calf, but he managed to stay on his feet.

"Ow," he groaned. "What're you doing?"

"Did you forget your promise?" Jaye demanded. Arms folded across her thin chest, she faced him from behind a clump of pines along the road to Bert's. "Now are you going to try to tell me you can't go to your imaginary job because you crashed your bike?"

"No, I—"

"I knew you'd try to get out of this, Jonah." Jaye turned her bike toward the general store. "Fooled you pretty good, didn't I? I bet you didn't even think I knew where this was." She tossed her braids and pedaled away down the sandy lane.

Jonah picked up his bike and rubbed the back of his leg. Why did things have to keep getting worse? It was like his first try at wiring a small motor in tech ed class. He'd been so excited, studying the schematic drawing and learning all of the parts. He'd stayed after school to finish. When Jonah had finished wiring the motor, he'd been so eager to flip the power switch that he hadn't checked over his work again. Sure enough, a crossed wire had caused a short circuit. The whole project had flamed out in front of his eyes, leaving his motor in a smoky ruin. Stealing the letter from school—that had been the first crossed wire. This lie about the job was another. What if Jaye was about to flip the switch and short out the whole summer?

* * *

"Just hold on, Jonah." Jaye wrenched her arm free. "You showed me some boats and docks. What does that prove? Where's the guy who gave you the job? In there?"

"Yeah, but he's probably busy. We'd better get you over to swim team, anyway." Jonah took Jaye by the arm again and tried to steer her back to their bikes. They hadn't run into Bert, Al, or Lenny. He glanced back over his shoulder. If only his luck would hold until he could get Jaye out of there.

"I thought so." Jaye refused to budge. "You don't want to go in," she said, peering at the faded letters on the side of the building, "because *Bert* has never even seen you before, has he?"

The front screen door of the general store swung open. With a sinking heart, Jonah watched Bert spit into the sandy dirt. The old man looked like he was wearing the same dirty undershirt he'd had on the day before.

"Someone callin' me?" Bert said.

This is the beginning of the end, Jonah thought. He glanced at Jaye. She was quiet now that Bert had come on the scene.

"Who's that?" Bert lifted his cigar at Jaye.

"My sister," Jonah mumbled.

"Eh?"

"My sister." Jonah heard his voice echo out over the water.

Bert looked hard at Jonah. He took a couple of quick puffs on his cigar. "Well, it's time to quit goofin' off. The power pack's gonna come in, and you've gotta get started on motor repair."

Jonah opened his mouth. No words came out. He stared at Bert.

Bert didn't even blink. "What? You got potatoes in your ears? The motor. You remember what a motor is, don't you?" He took his cigar out and spat again. "And look here, your sister can't be hangin' around. Take her over to wherever she was yesterday and get to work." Bert took a step back, then stopped, his hand on the door. "And you kin put this in that open flytrap of yours." He reached into his pocket and threw something their way. Then he stumped inside.

Jaye caught the two wrapped candies. She put the green sourball in her pocket and handed the red one to Jonah.

Jonah looked at his sister. He straightened his shoulders. "So, what do you think about my boss?"

"I'm going to swim practice." She hopped on her bike and rode off.

Before Jonah climbed on his bike to follow her, he looked back at the general store. He didn't know what to think about Bert, either.

CHAPTER 10

Jonah zoomed back down the access road to Bert's. He had barely said good-bye to Jaye. He hadn't even gotten off his bike to walk her down to the water. Fix a motor! He grinned to himself. Bert was going to let him fix a motor!

He ditched his bike next to the trucks and ran over to the black ski boat. The sleek 185 horsepower motor sat on its stand like a king on a throne. Its cover was back on it. Jonah ran his fingers along the cover's edge, stopping at one of the latches. Should he take the cover off and get the motor ready? He hooked his fingers under the latch's spring bar.

Jonah heard a door creak open. He pulled his hand away from the motor.

"Hey, airhead!" Al leaned out the open front door of the general store. "Bert wants you in back." The door banged shut.

Jonah took one last look at the motor and headed for the back of the store. He heard scrapings and crashes coming from the small shed. He pulled the open door wider and peered inside.

"Filthy stinkin' vermin," Bert swore. The old man was bent double with his back to Jonah. He was surrounded by newspapers stacked floor to ceiling. Empty crates like the ones Jonah had broken up the day before filled the rest of the cramped space.

Bert straightened. "Here," he said, thrusting a snarl of twine as big as one of the crates into Jonah's arms. "I got no time for this. You're gonna have to do it." He waved his hand at the stacks of papers, then pointed to a small pile bundled with twine. "These gotta go in my truck."

Jonah felt as if he'd been socked in the chest. "But you said—"

Bert scowled under his bushy eyebrows, stopping Jonah cold. "What I *said*..." He glared at Jonah. "What I *said* was you gotta pay your dues for what you did. *That's* what I said." With that, he swung the bundled stack past Jonah and stomped around the front of the store.

"There's got to be five years' worth of papers in this shed!" Jonah kicked at a pile. He stepped farther into the gloom, and the door swung shut behind him. The sour smell of the mouse droppings scattered across the floor almost choked him. He heaved the twine across the shed, sat down on a stack of papers, and put his head in his hands.

* * *

It was hours later when Jonah swung the last bundle of papers into the back of Bert's pickup. His arms ached all the way up to his shoulders, and his fingers were cut from the rough twine. The unforgiving sun had arced across the sky toward late afternoon. Jonah wiped his face on his shoulder.

"You're a worker, I'll give you that."

As if out of nowhere, Bert was standing next to Jonah. He held out a glistening bottle of soda.

Jonah accepted it without a word.

"Follow me," Bert grunted. He headed for the store.

Jonah stood where he was. "I can't start another job. I've got to go get my sister."

"I want to show you somethin'." The back door creaked open, then shut behind the old man.

"Right," Jonah said under his breath. "Can't wait."

He checked his watch. Actually he didn't have to be at the town beach for a good half hour. He took a long swig of soda and looked across the inlet to the barrier beach. A slate-gray workboat crossed the pond out beyond the cove. Jonah watched until it passed out of sight. Then he shrugged and walked to the door of the general store. Might as well see what he's got, he thought.

Lenny and Al sat planted on their stools in front of the small television. Bert leaned over the counter. His nose was practically touching a wide sheet of paper spread open like a map.

"Know how to read one of these?" Bert asked. He didn't look up.

"I don't think airheads can read," Al said, chortling.

"Give him a break, Pop," Lenny said. They went back to watching the soap opera on TV.

Jonah climbed onto the stool opposite Bert. The old man was examining a line drawing. It was a repair diagram for an outboard motor.

"I know how to read a schematic," Jonah said, leaning in closer. "I know about motors, too." He craned his neck, trying to see the schematic right side up.

"Hang on there," Bert said. "I'll turn it around for you if you promise not to drool all over it."

Jonah took the diagram over to the light coming through the back screen door. He recognized the spark plugs and carburetors, like parts in a car motor. Those parts were all in the top of the motor—the head. Jonah couldn't identify everything pictured in the lower unit. If only he could get his hands on an outboard, he'd be able to figure out the rest. He sat down on the floor and tried to work out the basics.

A sudden loud noise crackled above the drone of the TV.

"What the—?" Al was interrupted by the static again.

Bert held up his hand. He pointed to a black walkie-talkie on the shelf next to the TV.

"B...t," the radio sputtered. "C...ome...in...B...t."

The three men erupted in laughter.

"It's that college girl, isn't it?" Al slapped his knee.

"Yup," Bert nodded, chuckling. "Her professor gave her these walkie-talkies an' told her to set me up with one. I'm supposed to be keepin' an eye on her when she's out alone on the pond."

"Ah, let her go down with the ship." Al laughed. "That old workboat of theirs is runnin' on borrowed time any-ways."

Jonah wondered if hers was the gray boat he had seen crossing the pond earlier.

"Go down with the ship? Come on," Lenny said. "She can't go down far in that shallow pond."

"Lucky her. Why can't we get some of that luck?" Al complained. "First the bass are down and we don't have good fishing. Now she's out in the pond messing around with our scallops. Along with the eels, I'm counting on a good scallop season to get by, and so are you, Len. We don't need her out there screwing it up!"

Lenny looked at his father for a minute. Then he turned back to the soap opera.

The static crackled again.

Lenny pointed to the walkie-talkie. "You gonna answer that, Bert?"

Bert walked over and opened the front door. "Nah," he said from the doorway. "I'm not babysittin' that girl."

Jonah squinted at Bert, silhouetted in the doorway. "You don't think she needs help?" he asked.

"I kin see her from here. She's all right," Bert said. "Just testin' out her new toy radio is all."

"Will you all quit talking?" Al waved his hand at the TV. "I think they just said that guy is in a coma!"

"I'll keep my eye on her." Bert stumped over to Jonah and took the schematic from his hands. "Gimme this and get goin'. Tomorrow I'll show you somethin' you'll really go for."

Jonah was late. He rode like mad to meet Jaye. What a weird day, he thought. Up and down, up and down—like pumping on the pedals of his bike. He wondered what Bert was going to show him tomorrow. Jonah rounded a bend. He got a good view of the pond across the open fields of the park. He was relieved to hear the hum of the engine as he watched the gray workboat head back toward the marina.

CHAPTER 11

Opera music swelled from the cabin windows as Jonah and Jaye pedaled up the driveway. Exchanging a glance, they parked their bikes and opened the back door.

Uncle Nate leaned against the kitchen counter. Tears streamed down the sides of his long nose. His clasped hands were pressed to his chest as the singer's voice crescendoed in a glass-shattering note.

Jaye screwed her eyes shut and put her hands over her ears. Jonah grimaced. With a crash of symbols and a triumphant finish from the orchestra, the music faded away.

"Geez, Uncle Nate." Jonah stepped inside. "Maybe you'd better give this romance stuff a rest for a day or two."

Uncle Nate held a paper towel to his face and blew his nose with a loud honk. His shoulders shook. Just as Jaye reached out her hand to give Uncle Nate a pat, he whipped the paper towel off his face.

"Gotcha!" he shouted. He jumped away from the counter and pointed. The cutting board was piled with chopped onions.

Jonah pummeled his uncle's palms. Uncle Nate fended him off, laughing.

"Oh, you!" Jaye launched herself at Uncle Nate. He caught her and bounded into the living room with her.

"Nothing like good Italian opera to get you in the mood for pizza," Uncle Nate said. He dropped Jaye on the sofa and went to change the CD.

Pizza, Jonah thought? Did they even *have* pizza delivery around here?

"But for pizza, we need a little mood music." Uncle Nate put on another CD and began to sing, "When the moon hits your eye like a big pizza pie, that's *amore*." He waltzed Jaye around the room, tripping into the furniture with his gangly legs. Jaye's braids flew horizontal with each twirl.

Jonah shook his head. "Off the deep end," he muttered.

Uncle Nate let go of Jaye and came back into the kitchen. He took a dish towel off a large bowl and snapped it at Jonah.

"Here's what you need, Toolboy, too-cool-for-school boy," he said. "Make a fist."

He set the bowl in front of Jonah on the counter. Inside was a smooth pillow of dough.

"We're *making* pizza?"

"Certainly," Uncle Nate said. "What do you think this is, the land of twenty-four-hour delivery, like at your place? Now, wash your hands." Uncle Nate pointed at the dough. "Then punch."

Jonah soaped and rinsed his hands at the kitchen sink, then dried them on a dish towel. He balled his fist and slammed it into the dough—*thwack!* With a sigh, the pillow sank into a crumpled blob. Jonah looked up at his uncle in alarm.

Uncle Nate nodded. "Just right."

"I want to do that!" Jaye said.

"I've got another job for you." He dipped his hands into a bowl of oil, grabbed the flattened dough, and pulled it into three pieces. He tossed one piece to Jonah and another to Jaye, and demonstrated how to throw a ball of pizza dough into a pie circle.

"No, no, *no!*" he shouted as they tossed their dough in the air. "Not like that! You can't just *throw*. You have to *sing!*" He made them join in the song, throwing the dough up in the air in time to the music. "When the *moon* hits your *eye...*"

Jonah laughed so hard through the pizza making that the muscles in his stomach hurt. His mouth watered as the cabin filled with the yeasty smell of the dough, mingling with the aromas of tomato and melting cheese. Uncle Nate nearly ruined everything by telling all about what was going to happen to the star-crossed lovers in the next chapter of his romance. But even that didn't stop Jonah from enjoying the best pizza he'd ever tasted in his life.

* * *

After dinner they all got on their bikes and headed for the park. The day was cooling, the sun starting to dip behind the trees in the cove. Jonah watched his uncle's wild hair bounce up and down at the sides of his dome-shaped helmet. It didn't matter a bit that the park was just a field and some rusty swings. Uncle Nate was acting like his old self, the guy who could make being trapped in an elevator fun.

Sitting at the kitchen table after they'd finished the

pizza, Uncle Nate had described the unexpected idea that had helped him unstick a tough part of his novel earlier in the day. Jonah laughed, picturing his uncle jumping to his feet in the middle of his library research and shouting "Eureka!" or something equally goofy.

Maybe if I hang around Uncle Nate long enough, Jonah thought, I'll get an idea for that story I'm supposed to write. But getting an idea would involve actually thinking about the story. He shoved his bike into the old rack at the edge of the park. Not tonight, he decided.

Evening shadows crept across the field toward the playground. Uncle Nate leaned down and picked up a deflated football someone had left on the grass. Jaye hurried to catch up to him.

Two girls on swings drifted in lazy circles, toeing the sand under their feet. A boy sat on an upper rung of the jungle gym. His face, the pond, and the barrier beach far across it were lit with the last of the evening sun. The boy squinted down at Jonah.

"Is that a football?"

"Huh?" Jonah thought he recognized the boy from the swim team lineup the day before.

"You guys got a football?" the boy yelled to Uncle Nate and Jaye.

Uncle Nate turned. "Football?" he asked, as if that was the most ridiculous thing he had ever heard. "Why would I want a football? I have a *flatball!*" He waved the dead ball high in the air.

"Let me see it," Jaye said. She reached up toward his hand.

"Oh no, Jaye." Uncle Nate shook his head. "I can't let

just anybody have my flatball. Only certain people are able to hold it. It's not for everybody."

The girls stopped swinging and stood up. They watched as Jaye leaped toward Uncle Nate's hand. He continued to hold the flatball high out of her reach.

One of the girls took a few steps toward him. "Can I see it?" she asked.

Uncle Nate looked her up and down. "Sorry, no. I just don't see that happening."

The other girl walked over. "*Please,* may I see it?"

"I don't think so," Uncle Nate said with a sad smile.

The boy climbed down from the jungle gym. He ran toward Uncle Nate, then stopped and looked back at Jonah.

"It's just for boys, isn't it?" he said.

"Not for you two goofs," Uncle Nate said. "Best to keep away from it."

Jonah saw his uncle tense for a run.

"Let's get him!" Jonah yelled.

Uncle Nate bounded away on his long legs, the flat football held high over his head. With screams and shouts, every kid took off in pursuit. But not one of them, not even Jonah, could get a hand on the flatball. Uncle Nate climbed the jungle gym and jumped off. He dashed for the swings and launched through them. Around and around the park he went.

"I got him," the smaller girl yelled, grabbing the tail of his open shirt.

"Thanks!" Uncle Nate twisted out of his workshirt and ran off in his black T-shirt. "I was too hot, anyway."

They cornered him at the edge of the field, against a

stand of trees. He heaved the ball up into the air. It landed high in the crook of an oak tree. No amount of shaking would dislodge it.

"No fair!" the boy complained.

"All's fair in flatball," Uncle Nate announced.

Jonah flopped down onto the dry, scratchy grass. His sister and his uncle joined him. They gazed up at the first evening stars.

The other kids stared at the tree for a minute more. Then they gave up and went back to the swings.

After a while, Uncle Nate pushed himself up off of the ground. "Time to go, you two." He walked toward the bike rack, retrieving his other shirt from the ground on the way.

Jaye followed him, whining, "Do we have to go, Uncle Nate?"

"He's her uncle?" the boy asked Jonah.

"Yeah," Jonah said. "And mine," he added, bragging a bit.

The boy laughed at him. "KJ's your sister?"

"What?"

"KJ." He pointed at Jaye, standing with Uncle Nate by the bikes.

A car pulled up alongside the park on the pond road. The headlights blinked off and on.

"That's Dad," the boy said to the girls. "C'mon." He headed toward the car.

Jonah hopped on his bike and hurried after him. "Why do you call her KJ?" he asked.

The boy ducked into the waiting car. "Kiddie Jaye." He smirked. "We all call her that. No way that kid's twelve."

Jonah frowned, straddling his bike. The car pulled into the road, its headlight beams swinging across the dark trees. Jonah could see his sister and Uncle Nate riding up ahead. Jaye's shoulders poked bony and frail through her thin T-shirt.

"Hey, KJ's brother," the boy called out of the car window. "How come you're not on the team?"

Jonah didn't answer. The car's tires ground into the sand and pebbles at the edge of the road as the car pulled away. Jonah could taste the dust in his mouth. Looking at the two bicycles in the road ahead, there was no way for him to know whether Uncle Nate had heard that last bit about the swim team or not.

Uncle Nate and Jaye rode ahead. Crickets trilled, first one up in the leaves, then another behind a stump, then more and more of them, their music filling the dark spaces between the trees. Jonah heard the crunch of bicycle tires and the quiet murmur of voices on the gravel road in front of him.

When he reached the cabin, Uncle Nate was already in the kitchen making cocoa. Jonah was glad. On the slow, lazy ride back he had cooled down from all that running around. He ducked behind the curtain of his and Jaye's room to get ready for bed. Jaye was already under her covers, her knees and head supporting a tent. It was lit from inside by flashlight.

Jonah reached into his duffel bag for his own flashlight. He glanced up at his sister. She was still hidden under the blanket tent. Jonah reached into his bag again and checked under his toolbox. He felt all around the bottom of the duffel with his hand. As quietly as he could, he lifted the toolbox out and set it on the floor. He took each piece of clothing out and shook it. The letter from Mr. Ritchie was gone. Jonah froze.

"Jaye?" he whispered.

"Just a sec," she said. He heard the rustling of paper.

Jonah stood up and yanked away Jaye's blanket. "Give me that," he hissed. He grabbed the letter.

His hand was shaking. "What are you doing with this? We had a deal, remember?" He tried to keep his voice low. "I got you on the swim team, and you promised not to tell Uncle Nate about the letter. And that's the end of it, Jaye. Leave it alone."

"You're not just finishing a story," Jaye accused. "You're in a whole lot of trouble. Getting put in re...rem...in that other English class, and summer school, too. No way Mom and Dad know about this!"

"Okay!" Jonah said. "They don't. But I don't want to bother Uncle Nate about it. He has to write his book. I'll do the paper for Mr. Ritchie. It's nothing. Really—it's a snap." Jonah forced a smile. "You don't actually think I'm going into remedial English class, do you?" He made himself reach out to tug one of her braids.

"Cocoa's ready!" Uncle Nate called from the kitchen.

"Well, when are you going to work on your story?" Jaye said. She climbed down from her bunk. "Six pages is a whole lot, Jonah. You haven't done any of it yet, have you." That wasn't a question.

"Don't worry, I'll get it done," Jonah tried to sound more convincing than he felt. "Let's go get our cocoa." He pulled the curtain aside and nodded for her to go first. "It's going to be okay."

"What's going to be okay?" Uncle Nate asked.

Jonah pushed past Jaye. "She's afraid the cocoa will be too hot," he improvised. He felt her kick him. "I told her it would be okay."

"What?" Uncle Nate put his hands on his hips. "My cocoa too hot? It's perfect! Don't worry." He put his arm around Jaye's shoulders and guided her over to the counter. "Everything will be just fine."

"Yeah, I've heard that before." Jaye climbed on her stool.

Jonah reached over to give her a spin. She held on to the counter and wouldn't budge.

CHAPTER 12

When Jonah rode up the next afternoon, Bert was out on the dock filling a red gas can.

"Grab this." Bert swung the full can at Jonah. He replaced the pump nozzle and puffed on his cigar.

Jonah eyed the glowing stub and took a step away from the gasoline. "You wanted to show me something?"

Bert's parting words the day before were all Jonah had been able to think about. He'd even forgotten the KJ thing, at least until he'd seen the kid from the park over at swim team. But Jaye had seemed okay—fine, really. She'd ditched her towel and headed straight for the water. Jonah had decided to leave it alone.

"Thought you could have a look at this motor," Bert said.

Jonah couldn't believe his ears. He *was* going to get to work on the motor! He turned toward the place where the sleek black ski boat sat on its trailer. His view of the 185 horsepower motor was blocked by another boat, but Jonah knew it was there. Was Bert going to hook it to the gas can and try to start it up? Jonah hefted the can to his other hand and headed for the area with the trailered boats.

"Where're you racin' off to?" Bert was walking in the opposite direction. "It's over here."

Jonah watched Bert disappear around the back of the store toward the utility sink. He felt himself start a slow burn. How many times was Bert going to pull this, he wondered? Did he like torturing kids? He was probably laughing his head off right now, waiting at that sink full of foul dishes.

Well, this was going to be Bert's last trick. Jonah slammed the gas can down on the ground and marched after him. It was time to tell that cranky old man just what he could do with his third day's work. Jonah found Bert hunched over something on the ground next to the sink.

"Look," Jonah started.

"Yeah, get in here and have a look." Bert straightened and stepped aside.

At his feet lay a motor. A beat-up, grime-covered, beautiful, blue and white 25 horsepower Evinrude. So what if it wasn't the big 185 horsepower motor? Jonah sucked air through his teeth. He squatted down and put his hand on the crusty propeller.

"Yeah, take a good look at it. That's how a perfectly fine motor looks when someone don't treat it right," Bert said. "But I think it kin be fixed up okay."

Jonah ran his hands along the edge of the cover and snapped one of the latches open.

"Lissen," Bert said. "Don't spill its guts all over the ground. Haul it over to the lean-to an' put it on a stand. Then come in to get the schematic."

Jonah snapped the latch shut again and hoisted the

motor onto his knees. Hugging it to his chest, he stood up. It felt good and solid...and heavy.

"Hold it."

Jonah turned back to Bert. His knees sagged.

Bert looked off at the water and spat. "Prob'ly it'll take you a good chunk of time, but I'm betting you kin fix it. When I sell it, we're even on the power pack you broke." The old man disappeared into the store.

Jonah grinned. He staggered off toward the lean-to. Stepping up onto the cement slab floor, he heaved his burden onto an empty stand. He shook his aching arms. A built-in workbench lined the one solid wall of the lean-to. Jonah grabbed a heavy-duty socket wrench from an open toolbox. He held it by its socket head and gave it a spin. *Click-click-click-click-click*. Grinning all over again, he spun the wrench faster and faster, making a metallic whir all the way back into the store. When he stepped inside the back door, Lenny lifted a hand in his general direction without moving his eyes from the TV.

"Hey, airhead," Al called. "Bert wants to know what you did with his gas can."

* * *

The uneven chug of an approaching outboard drew Jonah's attention to the docks. He looked up from the Evinrude motor for the first time all afternoon. A battered wooden workboat nosed its way into a slip. Its captain leaped onto the dock, swinging her straight black hair out of the way as she fastened bow and stern lines to the dock's metal cleats.

Jonah leaned on the engine stand and watched the college girl step back aboard her boat. She was wearing shorts and wet suit booties. Her long legs were tanned a deep, smooth brown. She tossed things into a big bag and heaved the bag onto the dock. Then she unloaded some heavier gear. Jonah watched her move through the boat, securing lines. At the stern, she put one foot on either side of the motor, grabbed the top, and leaned back. The dripping propeller arced slowly out of the water until the motor clicked into tilt position.

It took several trips for the student to pack all of her belongings into a dinged-up blue van. She returned to the dock, sat down, and removed her wet suit booties. She leaned back on her hands and wiggled her toes in the hot sun.

"Gettin' anything done out here?" a gravelly voice boomed from the store.

Jonah jumped. Bert was leaning out the back door. He waved a bottle of soda.

Jonah accepted the drink. "I'm getting it all figured out first," he told him.

"Right," Bert said. "Just figure a little better'n you did on that other motor." He hunched over, shoulders shaking.

Jonah glanced at the student. She was too far away to notice the old man's choking-laughing fit. He took a swig of soda and looked at the Evinrude. He hadn't actually taken it apart, aside from removing the cover. Right off he had seen that the spark plugs were no good. Looking over the rest of the motor, Jonah knew that replacing those would be the easy part, and just the beginning.

He heard a rusty *scree* and a slam and looked up. The

blue van coughed and blared with the sound of a worn muffler. As the girl turned to back up, she waved. Jonah looked behind him, but Bert was no longer there. The sound of the van's engine receded, and Jonah watched a cloud of dust hang over the road, then disappear.

* * *

"Give me a sea turtle ride, Uncle Nate!" Jaye climbed on Uncle Nate's back. She screamed as he fell forward with a splash into the waist-deep water of the salt pond.

It was late that evening. From his perch against the beached skiff's gunwale, Jonah watched his sister and his uncle form a single silhouette on the surface of the pond. Sky and water faded to deep mauve. Their swimming motions created rings of black stippled with silver. Despite his fear of what might lurk underneath, the pond's surface seemed serene and gentle. The sound of ripples lapping at the shore was almost comforting.

The low hum of a far-off outboard brought Jonah's thoughts back to his Evinrude. It *was* his, at least until he fixed it to a purr and Bert sold it. That motor would be perfect on the back of a little skiff. Like the one he was sitting on.

Jonah got up and went around to the stern. He knelt and ran his hand along the dip in the gunwale—the cutout for the motor. That twenty-five horse would slide right in there. Jonah sighed. He had no idea how much the Evinrude would sell for when it was up and running. He did have some money—thirty dollars his mom had given him and twenty-four more he'd earned replacing the loose bolt lock and weather stripping on his neighbor's door. Fifty-four dollars seemed like a good bit of money. Jonah resolved to talk to Bert first thing the next afternoon.

"Jonah? You still out here?" Uncle Nate splashed up from the shallows, a long dusky shadow with a smaller shadow behind him.

Jonah stood up. "Over here."

"Figured out how to fix this thing up yet?"

"I'm working on it."

"That's one of the things I like about you, Toolboy." Uncle Nate put a cold, wet hand on Jonah's shoulder. He shook his head, sending out a spray of salty water. "Always working on something."

"I l-like your k-kind of work better, Uncle Nate," Jaye said, shivering. "T-tell us about your r-romance story. Are the p-people in love yet?"

"Not yet, my little Jaye-cicle," Uncle Nate laughed. He wrapped his towel around Jaye's shoulders and scooped her into his long arms. "They've just barely met. Let's go hop into pj's and I'll tell you all the juicy details." He turned to Jonah. "Coming in?"

"I think I'll stay out here a while longer," Jonah said. He climbed into the skiff.

"Not too big on romance, are you, Toolboy?" Uncle Nate asked.

"Not really," Jonah said. "But," he hurried to add, "I'm sure it's a great story."

He heard Uncle Nate chuckle all the way into the cabin. Jonah smiled, then felt with his fingers for the hole he had to patch.

CHAPTER 13

"Puh-le-e-eeze?" Jaye wheedled the next day. She parked her bike in the rack next to the pavilion and pulled a long face at Jonah.

"Oh, all right," he told her. "I'll watch your time trial. But I'm staying up here by the road. I have to head out to work as soon as your race is over."

"Thanks, Jonah!" Jaye clapped her hands. "I'm really fast—wait'll you see!" She hurried down to the water to join the other bobbing swimmers.

Jonah straddled the low seat and rolled his bike forward and back, watching his sister warm up. She is fast in the water, he thought. How would all of these older kids react if KJ—Kiddie Jaye—beat them? He checked his watch, wishing they'd get started.

The sooner she finished racing with her teammates, the sooner he could get to the marina and pitch his idea to Bert. It was going to be so great! He planned to patch up the skiff with the cans of stuff he'd seen under the black ski boat. When he finished repairing the Evinrude motor, he'd buy it for the skiff. He reasoned that Bert should give him a pretty good price on the motor since he was going to do the repairs himself. He'd have his own boat!

The coach blew his whistle, and a line of swimmers launched themselves freestyle toward the far rope. Jaye was already out in front. She executed a sharp turn and was halfway back across before her teammates finished theirs.

"Excellent time, Lander," the coach bellowed at the end of the race. "The rest of you—ten laps."

Jaye looked toward Jonah. He couldn't read her expression from where he was.

"Hey, look. It's the other one—the *big* Lander." The kid from the park pointed at Jonah.

"What *big* Lander?" The coach turned around.

Jonah spun his bike toward the road and took off. He didn't want to meet the swim coach. That could ruin everything.

As Jonah turned in the lane and coasted up to the general store, he was relieved to see that Al's red truck wasn't in front. But he couldn't find Bert, either. He wasn't out by the docks. And he wasn't behind the store. Jonah didn't even want to look at the Evinrude before he talked to Bert. He didn't want to jinx anything. He hurried through the back door of the store.

"Hey, airhead!"

Jonah's shoulders sagged. There was Al on his usual seat in front of the TV. A commercial about laundry soap was on.

"I didn't see your truck outside," Jonah said.

"Yah, well, Lenny took it up to Newburyport to sell our haul of eels."

Eels? Jonah shuddered involuntarily.

"By that look on your face I don't guess you'll be buying

any." Al slapped his knee. "Not too many people around here eat eels anymore, but the French go for them like crazy."

Jonah didn't care to hear about eating eels. He looked around the store. "Where's Bert?"

"He's out picking up parts. Whatsa matter—can't keep busy on your own?"

"I just need to talk to him is all."

"Whatever you need to know, ask me," Al said. "But not now. I'm watching my show."

The back of the store was a stockroom for spare parts. Jonah scanned the shelves, selecting two new spark plug wires and two plugs. He found a piece of paper and a pencil nub and started a list of materials to show Bert. Whistling, he took his loot out to the lean-to.

There was the Evinrude, right where he'd left it. Jonah removed its blue and white fiberglass cover and set it on the workbench behind him. He disconnected the shifting lever, then reached inside and pulled all the old spark plug wires off by their rubber boots. Using a spark plug wrench, he unthreaded the two corroded plugs. Their hook-shaped electrodes were burned. The choke and its butterfly flap were sticking, but it was nothing a shot of light machine oil couldn't fix. Jonah tested the flap, then cleaned it and retested it. He wiped it again, tapping the butterfly with his finger until it moved freely. Finally he screwed the two shiny new spark plugs in place and attached the new wires.

"Beautiful," Jonah said.

"Don't think you're done yet, do you?"

Jonah started. He looked over his shoulder. How long had Bert been standing there, he wondered? He hadn't even heard the truck drive up.

The old man took the cigar out of his mouth and spat into the bushes. He looked the motor over.

Jonah took a deep breath. "I've been thinking, Bert."

"Uh-oh," Bert grunted. "Here's trouble comin'."

"What's the—I mean, what—" Jonah stammered.

"Do you got somethin' to say or not?" Bert peered at Jonah from under his bushy white eyebrows.

"When I fix up the motor—"

"*If* you fix it," Bert corrected.

"When it's working—I mean—well, how much are you going to get for it?"

"How much am I goin' to get for it?" Bert's voice rose. *"How much am I goin' to get for it?* What—you're thinkin' maybe you don't owe me that much?" The cigar was going up and down at a furious pace. "Let me tell you somethin', mister, that power pack you broke—"

"No!" Jonah stepped back, waving his palms at Bert. "I don't mean that. What I meant to say—to ask—is can *I* buy it? I have this little skiff. Well, it has a hole. But I figured I could patch that—like you're doing to the black ski boat—and maybe I could buy the Evinrude when it's done. I'll fix it, then I'll buy it, see? I have fifty-four dollars."

The old man didn't say a word. He looked at Jonah for a long time. Jonah waited, heart pounding. Then Bert stared off into the distance. Jonah heard him draw in a long breath that ended in a hacking cough. But this time he didn't seem to be laughing.

"Can't do it," Bert said finally.

"But—"

"Look here," the old man interrupted. "Motor like

that'll bring in three-fifty, easy." He shook his head. "Can't let it go for your allowance."

"Three-fifty? Three hundred and fifty dollars?" Jonah's mind worked desperately. "I'll work for you all month," he blurted out. "You know I'm a good worker. I'll earn the money."

Bert shook his head again. "I kin pay you five an hour for odd jobs, but I only got enough for a few hours a week. Don't you have any other way to earn somethin'?"

"No," Jonah mumbled. He kicked a stone across the sandy ground.

"Well, you'd better keep at that motor, anyway." Bert scratched his bristly chin. "It's that next bit, the lower unit that'll show what you're made of." He went to the door, then turned back to Jonah. "Look, somethin' else could turn up. You never kin tell. Trollin' motor, maybe. A smaller one that you kin afford to buy." The door shut quietly behind him.

I don't want some puny trolling motor, Jonah thought. He ran his fingers over the new spark plug wires and flipped the butterfly flaps a few more times. He glanced at his watch. It was almost time to go and collect Jaye.

Jonah put the cover back on the Evinrude and fastened its latches. He took a rag and wiped down the cover. The motor already seemed different to him, special. If he had to explain it, he'd say the motor had come alive. He could already tell, with his fingers, what needed to be tuned and fixed. It was like he and the motor could communicate or something. Like the Evinrude was already his. He couldn't let Bert sell it away. He just couldn't.

Chapter 14

I think the rain is stopping, don't you?" Jaye asked early Monday afternoon. She craned her neck to see out the window from where she lay sprawled on the living room floor.

Jonah peered through the sheets of water sliding down the windows. The surface of the pond churned gray with the steady drumming of raindrops. Even a city boy used to the hiss of tires on soaked pavement could tell that this rain wasn't letting up anytime soon.

"I told you a hundred times, Jaye. This is an all-day kind of rain. It is a no-one-goes-in-the-water kind of rain. It's an if-you-ask-me-about-it-one-more-time-I-might-have-to-step-on-you kind of rain. No swimming today, get it?"

"But I didn't have swim team yesterday, or Saturday, either," Jaye said in a stage whisper. "We're getting ready for a meet!"

"You were in the water with Uncle Nate all weekend."

His sister had been born into the wrong family, that was all there was to it. There had been some incredible mix-up at the baby factory, and Jaye had shot out the wrong chute. Lander—Flounder—you could see how it had happened.

The back door banged. Uncle Nate came in from taking out the trash.

"Well, I'm not asking *you,* anyway," Jaye said. "I'm asking Uncle Nate."

"Asking me what?" Uncle Nate shrugged off his streaming rain jacket and stepped out of his boots.

"Don't you think the rain is going to end soon?" Jaye asked.

Jonah wrapped his fingers around an invisible neck and made strangling motions.

"Rain's not even slacking off," Uncle Nate said. "No, I'm afraid you'll have to be a Jayefish out of water today." He sat down on the couch and put his big feet up on the coffee table. He looked at Jonah. He pushed the table with one foot. Then he leaned over and poked his head underneath.

"No more rope around the legs?" Uncle Nate looked up at Jonah from under the table.

"No." Jonah crossed his arms over his chest. "No more rope."

"No more wobble?"

"Nope."

Winding rope at the bottom like some kind of crazy spider web—what kind of way was that to fix a table? Jonah shook his head. His uncle was hopeless when it came to repairs.

Uncle Nate heaved a long, drawn-out sigh. "Well, I guess I'll learn to live without the rope there somehow."

"You're not glad that Jonah fixed it?" Jaye asked.

Uncle Nate put his finger to his lips. "Let's let Jonah think he's getting away with something," he whispered.

Jonah looked at his sister in alarm. Did she know that Uncle Nate was teasing about his "getting away with" fixing the coffee table, and not about stealing the letter? Jaye gave Uncle Nate a goofy wink, and Jonah let out his breath. Getting away with things isn't all it's cracked up to be, he thought grimly.

Uncle Nate shook the coffee table again. It didn't even creak. "Looks like it's going to be a quiet afternoon at the old cabin," he said. He grabbed a book from the table and put his feet back up. "I guess I'll get some of this reading done," he said.

"If I can't go swimming, I'm going to make a story, just like you," Jaye said to Uncle Nate. "I think we *all* should." She raised her eyebrows at Jonah. Jonah looked out the window.

"Great!" said Uncle Nate. "What are you writing about?"

"Um...I think I'll write about my backstroke and butterfly stroke trophies."

Jonah groaned.

Jaye got her journal and colored pencils and flopped back onto the floor. Jonah rocked in the rocking chair. It creaked. He looked underneath it and noticed one of the rungs had come loose. Uncle Nate was reading. He looked like he was concentrating hard. Not a good time for repair work, Jonah decided.

Uncle Nate shifted in his chair. He jotted notes on a notepad. Jaye was coloring. Jonah sighed. Time to stop postponing the inevitable, he thought.

He padded across the floor to his room. The spiral notebook Uncle Nate had given him was buried in a pile of dirty clothes under his bunk. Jonah grabbed the notebook, took a pencil from the kitchen counter, and went back to the rocking chair.

At the top of the first blank page, he wrote *My Summer Story*.

He scratched his head. He held the pencil between his thumb and forefinger and jiggled it until it looked like rubber. He pulled the pencil along the inside edge of the page, letting the lead *tap-tap-tap* in a wavy line along the spirals.

Rain pelted the salt pond. Fat drops splashed back up into the air from the surface of the water like it was raining in two directions, down and up, down and up. Jonah traced the motion in the air with his finger. It made him think of tapping the carburetor flaps down and up on the Evinrude motor.

Jonah sketched the carburetor, the spark plugs, and everything he remembered from inside the head of the Evinrude. He drew a line around all of it for the cover and added the propeller shaft.

I would have gotten to work on the lower unit today if it wasn't for this stupid rain, he groused to himself.

"Done," Jaye announced. "Want to hear my story?"

Uncle Nate held up one finger, then traced it across the page he was reading.

"Come on, Uncle Nate," Jaye prodded.

Jonah could see that the rainy day wasn't helping his uncle, either.

"He has to read," Jonah told Jaye.

"No, no. That's okay." Uncle Nate took a last look at his

book and closed it. He smiled at Jaye. "Ready," he said.

"There was once a girl named Star," Jaye began. "Star was the very fastest swimmer in the world."

"And quite modest, too," Jonah said.

"Is this your story or my story?" Jaye demanded. She held up her notebook to show a picture of a girl with dark braids standing next to a giant trophy.

"Star loved to swim in races every day," Jaye continued. "She finished her first race in one minute and twenty seconds." Jaye held up a new picture of the girl standing next to another trophy. She turned the page. "Her second race time was one minute and fifteen seconds. And her next race..."

Jonah's thoughts drifted. Through the window he could see the skiff sitting at the water's edge. There was the notch for the motor, the place where the Evinrude would tuck right in. He continued to sketch idly in his notebook.

"...and she won the Olympics and they named the biggest swimming pool in the world after her. The end." Jaye snapped her notebook shut and beamed. "How do you like it?"

"That's quite a story there," Uncle Nate said. "Quite a story." He clambered down onto the floor next to her. "Is it done? Anything you'd like to add to it?"

Jaye leafed through her notebook. "Well," she said. "All of the pictures of Star and her trophies do look sort of the same." She turned to the first page again. "Do you think something else should happen? Hey, can I make it into a romance? Like yours?"

"Sure." Uncle Nate grinned. "Who's the love interest going to be?"

"Well," Jaye said. "There's this boy on the swim team…"

Jonah pretended to gag.

"Whoa there, Jayefish," Uncle Nate held up his hands. "Let's stick to fiction, or your parents'll have my head!"

"I didn't mean a *real* boy on my *real* swim team," Jaye said. Jonah thought her cheeks looked a bit pinker than usual.

"All right then." Uncle Nate rubbed his hands together. He looked like he was enjoying himself. "How will the girl and boy get thrown together? In a good romance, they have to notice each other right away. Let's see if we can set up that part of the story first."

"Do they have to like each other right away, too?" Jaye asked.

"Oh, no," Uncle Nate said. "If they don't like each other at first, that can make the romance even more exciting." He wiggled his eyebrows.

Jaye giggled.

They bent their heads over her notebook and started trading ideas. Jonah watched them, then went back to his drawing. After a minute or two, Jaye looked up at Jonah.

"Yours is next," she told him.

Jonah looked down at his own open notebook. He had not written any of *My Summer Story*. Not a word. What he had done was draw a perfect sketch of the skiff, with the Evinrude fitted snugly into the stern.

Jonah had no story. He was going to be in remedial English for the rest of his life. And worse, he had no way to earn three hundred dollars. The Evinrude motor was never going be his.

CHAPTER 15

"Didn't figure you for one of those fair-weather workers." Bert squinted at Jonah, one bushy eyebrow raised. "Thought you'd be workin' on that Evinrude yesterday, rain or no. Here." He held out an empty outboard tank and motioned toward the gas pump.

Jonah grabbed the tank. "I've got other stuff to do when it rains," he mumbled. Stuff like staying home pretending my swim team was cancelled for the day, he thought. He emptied a can of oil into the tank and began to fill it from the pump.

"Didn't think a truckload of candy bars'd keep you outta here." Bert scratched his chin. "Anyways, bring that can over to the store when you're done an' you kin get right to work."

"What work?" Jonah said.

"*What work?* I'm talkin' about the Evinrude. You don't think that motor's ready to go, do you?"

"But I want to do the other work first." Jonah struggled to keep his voice steady. He looked down, his eyes on the gas tank. "The work for pay, I mean. You said you had some for me."

Bert was quiet for so long that Jonah looked up just to make sure he was still there. The old man was staring across the cove, the cigar in his mouthing working up and down. He turned to Jonah.

"I see what you're gettin' at. But I don't want you to get your hopes all up—"

"I just want to try," Jonah said. He slammed the pump's nozzle back into its cradle. "Just let me try, okay?"

"Well," Bert took his cigar out and spat. He looked over at the docks. "I got a job, but you're not gonna like it."

Jonah screwed the cap on the outboard tank and followed Bert to the water's edge. A heap of floats attached to a snarl of green-slicked ropes lay drying in the sun. Jonah pulled the collar of his T-shirt over his nose against the low-tide stench of decay.

"Hauled these moorin' floats out over the weekend." Bert indicated the pile with his cigar. "They need a good scrubbin' before I kin put 'em back in the water."

The floats were stuck together with hairy mats of green seaweed growing over layers of barnacles. There were jelly-like things, too. Plants or animals? Jonah wasn't sure. Small black flies buzzed in and out of the pile. Jonah waved his hand around his head.

"Fine, I'll do it." His voice came out muffled behind his shirt.

"C'mon then," Bert grunted. "I'll get you the cleanin' stuff."

Jonah picked up the gas tank and followed him back to the store. Lenny and Al were in their seats at the counter, eyes glued to the TV. Jonah traded Bert the red tank for a bucket and a scraper.

"Have fun, kid," Lenny yelled after him as Jonah banged out the screen door.

"Yeah, you too," Jonah muttered. "Keep up the good work."

He filled the bucket from the hose out front and trudged to the heap of floats. He wanted to take off his T-shirt and tie it over his nose, but decided against it. Who knew what was growing on those things? What if something from that pile slapped against his chest—something with stingers? Jonah winced. He'd just as soon not touch any of it. But getting even a little money for the motor had to be worth the risk. He gritted his teeth and forced himself to reach for the nearest float.

"Hey, airhead!"

Jonah jerked his hand back. He turned just in time to get hit in the chest with a pair of black gloves long enough to cover his elbows.

"What're you, crazy?" Al laughed at him. "Them barnacles'll rip your fingers to shreds! Good thing I came back out here to finish repairs on my eel traps." Al shook his head. His footsteps rang along one of the docks.

* * *

Jonah straightened up and wiped his forehead on his shoulder. The water had receded, baring a cobble of dark mussels wedged between green rocks. Bladders of brown seaweed bobbed on the tiny wavelets washing into the cove. Jonah's shadow reached the water's edge, the sun at his back heading down the sky toward the trees. Al and Lenny had driven away in the red truck at least an hour earlier. Home in the city, he'd never thought of reading the shadows. Here he knew it was almost time to get Jaye from swim team.

The pile of floats didn't look a whole lot smaller. Maybe if he pushed it he could clean a couple more before he had to go. He needed the heap of clean ones to be bigger than the ones he'd still have to face the next day. The sound of an outboard approaching the marina reminded him of his Evinrude motor. Maybe tomorrow I'll have time to work on it, he thought.

He yanked two floats free of the pile. Scrubbing one furiously, he sent pieces of barnacles and algae flying in all directions. A mud-colored blob hit him in the eye with a squish.

"Aaugh!" he yelled. His mouth tasted of salty grit.

He grabbed for the hose and turned it on his face. Did Bert stay up nights inventing these disgusting jobs, he fumed, or was everything that had to do with the pond completely repulsive?

As he rubbed his eye with the bottom of his shirt, he heard a heavy clang and then scraping sounds from far out on the dock. He glanced up. The college girl was hauling a large plastic crate toward her van, her long, dark ponytail swinging from side to side.

Jonah went back to his work. He heard a crash. Over in the parking area, the crate lay on its side, its contents dumped onto the sandy gravel. The girl heaved the crate up into the open back of her van and began tossing in her spilled equipment.

Jonah checked his watch. Maybe I'll start off tomorrow on the Evinrude, he thought, just for a few minutes. He shut his eyes against the spraying debris and scrubbed the last float as fast as he could. He heard the screen door of the store slam and then footsteps crunching over the gravel.

"Got something against that float?"

Jonah opened his eyes. The college girl stood in front of him, her hand shading her brow. He glanced back over his shoulder.

"You," she said. "I'm talking to you."

Jonah looked down at the half of a float left in his hand. He felt his face go red. "It's fine," he said flatly and tossed the mangled float on the clean pile. What's it to her, anyway, he thought.

"Hey, lighten up—I'm kidding. I came over to talk to you about giving me a hand."

Jonah glanced toward her van. She'd already packed away her tangled pile of equipment.

"Is it quick? I have to clean this up and go," he said. He dumped the bucket at the water's edge, then started spraying the bucket and gloves with the hose.

"I didn't mean today. I need someone to crew with me most afternoons. One of my lab partners was going to do it, but now he can't start until August. Of course, if you'd rather scrape floats…"

Like anyone wanted to scrape these slimy floats. Jonah flung the gloves into the bucket. He couldn't waste time hauling things around for this college girl, though. His motor was waiting for him. And right now, Jaye was waiting for him.

Jonah picked up the bucket by its handle. "Sorry. I can't help you," he said, turning to go. "I have to work for Bert."

The girl grabbed the bucket's handle, jerking him to a

stop. The caramel skin of her arm was streaked with white from dried saltwater. She swung her hair over her shoulder in a fluid motion, her dark eyes meeting Jonah's angry look.

"That's kind of funny," she said. "Because Bert's the one who sent me out to talk to you. He said you're looking to earn some money. I told him I've got enough in my grant to pay ten an hour." She let the bucket handle go. "But if you're not interested, never mind."

She spun on her heel and strode off, her wet suit booties smacking the gravel in a rapid tattoo.

Ten dollars an hour? Jonah's thoughts were spinning. The girl climbed up into the battered blue van.

Jonah wanted time to work on his Evinrude, too. But ten dollars an hour! The van backed up.

Jonah started to run. "Hey!" he yelled.

The van lurched down the lane. Jonah dashed for his bike.

"Hey!" he yelled again. He rode up and pounded on the van's back door. "Stop!"

The van slowed to an idle. He crashed through the brush to the side window. The college girl turned to him from the driver's seat. Her eyes were hidden behind mirrored sunglasses.

"Need something?"

"The job," he gulped. "I need the job."

"One o'clock tomorrow," she said. She gunned the motor and was gone in a spray of gravel.

"I can't be here right at one," Jonah called after the van. "I have to take my sister to swim team." His voice hung on the air like the dust from the road.

CHAPTER 16

The next afternoon, Jonah stood on the pedals and pumped as fast as he could toward the marina. Why had Jaye dragged her feet on the way to swim team today of all days? He heard an outboard motor start up.

He skidded to a stop in the parking area. A boat was pulling away from the dock. He could see the college girl's back, her hand easing the throttle forward. Her hair whipped around her narrow shoulders like a banner in the breeze. She nosed the bow away from the moored boats, heading for the open pond.

"Hey!" Jonah shouted. "Hey, wait!"

She didn't turn around. The motor was running high and rough as the work skiff moved farther and farther away. She'd never hear him now.

Jonah grabbed a handful of gravel and flung it at the ground, pelting the aluminum dock in a ringing spray. He had tried to tell her yesterday that he couldn't get there exactly at one. She hadn't heard him. What if she took back the job offer? If Jonah didn't come up with enough money, Bert was going to sell the Evinrude to someone else.

The bucket, scraper, and gloves were sitting where he'd abandoned them the day before. Jonah gave the whole show a furious kick. The bucket spiraled down the beach and crashed into the heap of floats. Stomping down to the pile, Jonah grabbed the bucket. He wound his arm overhead to throw it. He felt someone looking at him and turned in a fury.

"When you're done scrapin', put that bucket an' gear where they belong." Bert was leaning in the doorway of the general store. "Put 'er away, and put 'er away clean. Bert's law." He turned and went inside.

Jonah could feel the blood pounding in his face. He lowered the bucket to his side, his knuckles white on the handle. The former contents of the bucket lay in a trail down the beach. One glove pointed at the heap of mucked-up floats as if to say: *this is your job*. He might as well forget about high-paying boat rides. He had the disgusting job, the one that would never pay enough to buy the Evinrude. Jonah slogged up the beach to collect his equipment.

* * *

Jonah heard the crunch of Bert's footsteps and straightened, wiping his face with his shirt.

"You earned this," Bert said. He held out an icy root beer.

Jonah tossed the last float onto the clean pile and accepted the sweating bottle gratefully. He tipped back and took a long swig, letting the sweet bubbles scour the taste of salty decay from the back of his throat.

"Look here, kid," Bert said. "Sumi's havin' some sort of boat trouble out there." Bert pointed his cigar out to the left of the cove.

"Who?" Jonah asked.

"Sumi. That college girl. I don't quite make her out on the walkie-talkie. Think you kin run out in the Whaler an' see what she needs?"

Jonah almost choked on his soda. "M-me?"

"I'm waitin' on a call about some parts, an' Lenny and Al are out after bass. You've run a boat before, right?"

Should he tell Bert he'd only been boating a few times? What if he got to the college girl and didn't know what to do to help her? He looked at the docked boats. The big outboard motors gleamed in the sun.

"Sure," he told Bert.

A new set of creases appeared at the corners of Bert's blue eyes. He tossed Jonah a key on a small float and went back up the narrow beach. "Tow her boat in if you gotta," he called over his shoulder.

Tow her in? Jonah stared at the key in his hand. He was going to drive a boat! He broke into a slow, wide grin. Then he ran out onto the dock. He looked at all of the boats, his heart racing. First he had to figure out which boat was the Whaler.

* * *

The Whaler was named "Bert's Buddy." That was a pretty good tip-off. A fat coil of towrope lay in the stern, along with a set of oars, a toolbox, and a spare gas can. Jonah untied the lines, then pulled the Whaler around the other docked boats by its bow line. Once he had to jump into a boat to keep the Whaler from banging into it. Jonah hoped Bert wasn't watching.

When he reached the end of the dock, he climbed into the Whaler and pushed off with his foot. His palms were so sweaty, he nearly dropped the key. I can do this, he told himself. He managed to get the key in the ignition and turned it. The motor made a terrible noise and belched smoke. Jonah jerked the key back to the off position. He hadn't remembered to put the propeller into the water. The boat drifted back toward the dock. Luckily for the nearby boats, he hadn't remembered to take in the fenders, either. He hauled them into the boat and went back to the motor. He pulled it back to free it from its tilt position, let the propeller drop into the water, and turned the key again. This time it started easily.

Jonah stood at the small console and eased the Whaler toward the mouth of the cove, the propeller churning underwater behind the boat. He tried to go slowly and learned a quick lesson in seamanship. The slower he went, the harder it was to get the boat to turn.

Soon his left hand on the wheel started to feel the outgoing tide and the crosscurrents pushing and pulling at the rudder. His body was beginning to channel the information to his right hand on the throttle. He let the speed control the boat's movement through the water. The cove widened. Jonah nosed the throttle forward. The Whaler picked up speed, its bow rising.

Whoa, he thought. Not bad.

As he came out into the open pond, a salty sea breeze hit Jonah's face and the currents pulled harder. The water sparkled under a jewel-blue sky. Tiny whitecaps danced by. Far across the pond, he saw the silhouette of the college girl's workboat.

Jonah looked over his shoulder. Then he hit the throttle forward all the way. The Whaler's bow lifted out of the water and the boat shot ahead.

"Wahoo!" Jonah whooped. He grabbed for the console and braced his legs.

"Awk, awk," called a passing gull.

"Look at me!" Jonah yelled back. "*I'm* flying!"

The Whaler tore across the pond. Jonah could see the college girl, Sumi. She was waving. He waved back. She'll be glad I came to get her, he thought. He'd zoom in close, then cut his motor right at the last minute. When she saw how he could handle a boat, she'd be sure to give him the job.

The workboat's anchor line was out. It looked curiously slack, almost horizontal. Now the college girl was pointing. *Into the water*. Then she was flapping her hands up and down. Jonah didn't care what was down there. He wasn't a water guy. He was a boat guy.

He was nearing the skiff, only about fifty feet off. The girl held her palms out toward him. He rolled his eyes. Did she think he was going to crash into her? He knew what he was doing. Her mouth was moving, but he couldn't make out her words over the roar of his motor. Then Jonah saw the top of her anchor sticking out above the water. He gasped.

He hauled back on the throttle and tried to throw the motor into reverse. He was too late. He cut the motor just as the propeller struck sand. Jonah raced back to the stern to yank the prop out of the water. Then the front hull ran aground. The high wake following him grounded him more firmly still.

"Way to go for that sandbar!" the college girl shouted.

Elation drained out of Jonah like water from a punctured radiator. He turned his back on her.

"You can probably just hop out and push off," she said.

Without turning, Jonah looked over the side. Crabs scuttled across the sand, and a dark shadow darted through the water. No way, Jonah thought. I'm not getting in that. And I don't need her to tell me what to do.

"If it's too heavy for you to push off," he heard the girl call to him, "you can just wait. Bert's sending someone out for me."

Jonah groaned inwardly. He grabbed one of the oars lying in the bottom of the Whaler and shoved it against the sandy bottom as hard as he could. The boat didn't budge.

"You'd be better off out of the boat," the girl said.

Jonah ignored her. He stood in the bow and pushed with the oar. He lost his balance and slammed his elbow on the gunwale. He stood again and heaved on the oar. He thought the Whaler shifted a bit toward the deeper, darker water off the sandbar. Small waves nudged it back.

Jonah doubled his efforts. He willed the boat to move, leaning all of his weight into the oar. Nothing. Then he had an idea. Instead of standing in the grounded bow, he went toward the stern of the Whaler. Digging the oar into the sandbar, he pushed the boat backwards and jerked his weight toward the stern. Inch by inch the Whaler slid off the sandbar. Jonah shot an angry glare at the workboat. Then he dropped the motor in and started it up.

Giving the sandbar a wide margin, he motored slowly around it to the girl's boat. She was sitting near the bow on a box built into the bulwark. Maybe I can just do what I need to do without having to talk to her, Jonah thought.

He flipped the Whaler's fenders over the side and tossed a line into her boat.

"What are you doing?" Sumi asked. She let the line slide off her gunwale into the water.

"Taking a look at your boat," Jonah answered through clenched teeth. He reached across with the oar and pulled the Whaler in close to the workboat. Then he tied up with one of his lines.

"I told you Bert's sending someone."

"Yeah." Jonah stepped into the wooden boat. "Me."

"You?" She burst out laughing. "You're joking, right? Aren't you the kid who *doesn't* work?"

"I work for Bert," Jonah said. He put his hand on the gunwale, ready to climb back aboard the Whaler. This girl didn't want his help. After his demonstration on the sandbar, she didn't think he could handle a boat anyway. She didn't even think he was responsible enough to show up for work.

But he couldn't just leave her. For one thing, Bert had trusted him with the Whaler and expected him to help out. Even more important, Jonah needed to show this girl that he knew how to fix things—that he *could* help.

He'd loved that feeling of flying across the pond. He wanted a boat of his own. If Jonah fixed her boat, maybe this college girl would hire him after all. He went to her console table and turned the key.

"Tried that," Sumi said.

Jonah didn't listen to her. He was listening to the motor. It coughed but wouldn't turn over. "Sounds like it's out of gas."

"It's not," the girl said.

Jonah picked up the gas can. It felt heavy enough to be about half full. That's odd, Jonah thought. He checked the connection between the gas tank and the black hose that fed gas into the motor. Then he took the cover off the motor and found where the hose connected inside. Everything looked okay. He picked up the gas can again and shook it. He opened the can's cap and poured a bit of gas into his hand. He stared at his hand, then sat back on his heels.

"Where'd this gas come from?" he asked.

"It's the spare I had here. I filled it at school the day before yesterday," Sumi said. She moved to the stern and stood over Jonah. "Why?"

Jonah stood up. He hadn't realized how small she was, barely taller than Jonah himself. He held out his cupped hand. "Looks like what's in my hand is mostly water, with some gas floating on top."

"What?" She took off her sunglasses and peered at his hand. She touched the liquid, then rubbed her fingers together. She stared. "It *is* mostly water. But how could that be?"

"Something wrong with the pump at your school?"

"Not that I know of."

Jonah shrugged. "Anyway, the motor's not going to run now. Can't burn water for fuel."

The girl closed her eyes for a minute. "This can't be good for the motor." She shook her head.

"I bet there's no real damage," Jonah said. He'd learned about what would happen if water got into the gas from his tech ed teacher at school. "The water just has to be drained out of the system is all."

"If I can't start the motor, how am I supposed to get back to the dock?"

"I can tow you."

Sumi stood up and put her sunglasses back on. "But not over the sandbar, right?"

Jonah gritted his teeth and hopped back in the Whaler.

"I was kidding," Sumi said.

Without another word, Jonah tied the heavy towrope from his stern to the bow of the work skiff. He started up the Whaler and began the ride back to the marina.

"There's a big rock over there," Sumi yelled from the workboat.

"Don't go that way," she added. "The eelgrass is too thick."

A few minutes later she called, "Stay in the channel."

Instead of thanking me, Jonah fumed, she just has to keep telling me what to do. But he thought he'd better pay attention to what she was saying about the hidden land-scape under the glistening water, just the same.

* * *

"Can you do it?"

Jonah had left the workboat at its usual slip and was tying the Whaler in its own place at the dock.

"I'm fine," he said over his shoulder. "I can tie up a boat."

"No. I'm asking if you can fix my motor."

Jonah turned slowly. Sumi stood on the dock above him. Her eyes were hidden behind the dark glasses, but a small smile creased the corners of her mouth.

"You want me to work for you?"

"I've got a ton of work and I'm working against a deadline. But you can't show up late."

"I tried to tell you yesterday," Jonah said. "I have to take my sister to swim team at one." He stepped up onto the dock next to her. He saw Bert watching them from inside the store. "I can get here by one-fifteen."

"You can do the motor tomorrow, right?"

"Yes."

"What's your name, anyway?" she asked.

"Jonah."

She smiled. "Like the guy who got swallowed by a whale?"

He didn't answer. He'd only heard that one about a thousand times before.

"I'm Sumi." She stuck out her hand. "See you tomorrow at one-fifteen."

Her fingers were small and thin, but her handshake was strong. She walked to her van and drove off in a curtain of dust.

Jonah looked out across the pond. Sunlight played off the ripples near the barrier beach. He closed his eyes and was back in the Whaler, flying across the water with the salt air in his face. He thought about the Evinrude motor waiting for him in the lean-to and raised both fists in the air.

"Yes," he whispered. "Yes!"

CHAPTER 17

"Jaye, come *on!*" Jonah banged back into the cabin to look for his sister. She wasn't in the kitchen stuffing snacks into her pack. She wasn't in their room digging for her swim gear.

"Jaye?"

"Wha...?" came a phony sleep-filled voice from the living room couch. Jaye sat up. She made a big show of rubbing her eyes.

"Listen, fake-a-roni," Jonah said, "it's almost one. Uncle Nate's gone already, and we have to get you over to swim team."

Jaye stretched her arms toward the ceiling. "But I'm too tired," she said, yawning.

Jonah grabbed her hands and pulled her to her feet. "What's with you? We have to leave now."

Jaye flopped back onto the couch. "I can be late."

"I can't." Jonah went to find Jaye's pack. He hauled her up off the couch again and propelled her toward the back door.

"Come on, Jonah." Jaye shuffled slowly. "It's not like Bert stands there waiting for you with a stopwatch."

"I'm not working for Bert today," he said. Jonah explained to Jaye about his new job as Sumi's assistant. "*She* waits with a stopwatch."

"You mean you get to go out on a boat?" Jaye asked. She followed Jonah out the door.

Jonah grinned. "Yeah. I even got to drive a boat," he said.

Jaye didn't say much on their ride around the pond. When they got to the town beach, the swim team was already warming up. Jonah looked at his watch. It was one-ten. "Well, 'bye," he said to Jaye.

"I want to go with you," she said.

Jonah filled his cheeks and blew an impatient breath. "You can't, Jaye," he told her. "I'm just working on a motor today, anyway. You wouldn't like it. This college girl's pretty bossy. She gives more orders than Mom and Dad put together."

"Mom and Dad are going to kill you when you get home." Jaye's lower lip trembled slightly. She put her bike in the rack and headed down the beach. Her shoulders drooped under her pack.

Jonah watched her go. I shouldn't have mentioned Mom and Dad, he thought. Jaye was probably more than a little homesick. She was only ten, after all. Just a little kid. He leaped back on his bike and sprinted for the marina.

Jonah didn't want to think about his parents, either, but not because he was homesick. He hadn't done anything about the story for Mr. Ritchie. He didn't even have any ideas for it. He missed his parents, too, but he was starting to dread their return. Stealing the letter had gotten him to Uncle Nate's, and his lies had kept him out of the pond so far. But still, when August came Jonah was going to be in big, big trouble.

He shook those thoughts out of his mind and pedaled harder.

* * *

When Jonah reached the marina, Sumi was already on the dock organizing gear. Her long hair was clipped on top of her head, and she wore a green T-shirt that said "Nature Is." He walked out onto the dock.

"You're late," she observed.

Jonah checked his watch. It was one-seventeen. She stood and bent to pull something from a gear bag behind her. The back of her T-shirt said *In Charge*.

No kidding, Jonah thought.

"Get started, why don't you?" she said, without turning around.

"I've got to ask Bert about your motor," he said. "I'll be right back."

He walked up to the general store and stuck his head in the door. In the dim light he saw Lenny and Al sitting on their stools. Bert's rag traced circles on the scratched countertop.

"So, no good, eh?" Bert was saying to Al.

"Nah." Al didn't move his eyes from the TV screen. "Out since three this morning. Couple a bass. Nuthin' to speak of."

"You do all right with them eels?" Bert asked Lenny.

The young man nodded. "Yeah. I'm going out tomorrow

to check the traps Pop fixed." He blew a big bubble and sucked it back in with a snap.

Bert noticed Jonah. "Whaddya need, kid?"

"I need to know how to get water out of a motor."

Al guffawed. "Sunk a boat already, airhead?"

"It's not my boat," Jonah said. He turned back to Bert. "It's Sumi's."

Bert stopped wiping the counter. "The motor went under? That was the problem yesterday?"

"It didn't go under," Jonah said. "But it wouldn't start. Some water in the gas, maybe."

"Tough break," Lenny said.

"Could you keep it down?" Al said. "I missed what they just said about that guy's coma."

Lenny grinned and blew a bubble with his gum.

Bert walked Jonah out the back door.

"Salt or fresh water in the gas?" Bert asked.

"Fresh, I think."

Bert took off his cap and scratched his head. "Well, first off, you gotta take out your spark plugs an' your carburetor." He ticked off the tasks on his stubby fingers. "Give it a shot of that carburetor cleaner I have out by the lean-to. Empty the tank an' get new gas to flush the lines. Clean the fuel filter. Then put it all back together—new plugs— an' start it up. Let it run a while to dry out."

"Doesn't sound too bad," Jonah said, more to himself than Bert. Actually it sounded great.

"Don't forget the bit where you cross your fingers an' toes an' hope it don't blow up." Bert put his cigar back in his mouth and looked at Jonah.

Jonah looked at Bert in alarm. The old man bent double and gasped, his round shoulders shaking. When Jonah walked away to get the tools he needed, Bert was still laughing.

* * *

Jonah stepped over the array of nets, scoops, metal squares, and other odd-looking science gear Sumi had on the dock. He climbed aboard the workboat. Its flat bottom left lots of room for worktables and other built-in equipment.

"What's this for?" He pointed to a motorized spool of heavy wire cable.

Sumi put a ruler down to mark the place on the map she'd been studying. "It's a winch," she said. "The switch and the lever on the side control the cable winding in and out. It's for towing sampling nets. When I pull the net in, I hook it to that davit." She gestured toward a four-foot-high metal arm with a huge wooden pulley on the end. "Then I dump the sample onto the table underneath." The table was like a big open box on legs. "This side of the table slides out," she said, pointing to the outside edge of the box, "so when I'm done I can wash everything back into the pond."

"Cool." Jonah tugged on the pulley, and the davit swung toward him with a sudden, high-pitched squeal. He ducked. The pulley lurched by his head.

"Watch it. The davit is supposed to be tied back when it's not being used." She stepped into the boat and tied a line from the davit to a cleat near the deck. The rope held the metal arm snugly in place. "So...the motor?" she said. She turned and stepped back out of the boat. Jonah saw the words on the back of her shirt again—In Charge.

"Right," Jonah said. At the boat's stern he grabbed the top of the motor and leaned backward, tilting it out of the water.

"Put the motor cover on the worktable," Sumi told him.

Jonah unclipped the cover and set it on the table next to the davit. He'd been planning to put it there anyway.

When he pulled out the wet spark plugs she said, "I don't think you should force those like that."

Jonah gritted his teeth. If she knew anything about spark plugs, she'd be fixing the motor herself. Why didn't she go back to her own work?

She leaned over the gunwale as he struggled with the carburetor. "Are you sure that comes out?" she asked.

The sun baked Jonah's back through his T-shirt. Lines of sweat snaked down the sides of his face. "Could you—"

"See ya, airhead," Al yelled, coming outside. He climbed into his red truck and slammed the door. Lenny stuck his arm out the other window and waved as they drove off.

"What's that he called you?" Sumi asked.

Jonah winced. "Nothing." He went back to the carburetor.

"I don't think that comes out," Sumi said again.

A slight breeze lifted the corner of her map. It slid along the dock. Sumi hurried away to get it.

"In the store you could spread your map on the counter," Jonah observed.

"It's called a chart." She sat down next to the boat and jotted notes on a clipboard.

Now maybe she'll leave me alone so I can work, Jonah thought. Sumi's back was to him. He saw her tap her pencil against her chin. Strands of her long hair had escaped the clip and made graceful trails down her neck. Jonah watched her wind the strands around her fingers. Then she undid the clip, shook out her hair, and pinned it up high on her head once again. When she turned, Jonah quickly looked back down into the motor.

He sprayed the carburetor with cleaner and drained the bad gas out of the lines. When he finished cleaning and replacing parts, Jonah refilled the gas tank and squeezed the priming bulb. Pulling back on the motor, he released the lock and let it down into the water. The key was in the ignition. He looked over his shoulder at the door of the general store and crossed his fingers.

The motor coughed once, then twice, in a billow of smoke. Then it started with a wonderful, deafening roar.

"I don't believe it!" Sumi yelled.

Why'd she even ask me to do the job, Jonah wondered, if she didn't think I could? He leaped onto the dock and stomped toward Bert's. "It has to run for at least half an hour to dry out," he shouted over his shoulder.

"Okay, you can go then," Sumi called after him.

"In Charge," Jonah muttered. He fished in his pocket for change and bought a soda. He still had an hour or so until he had to get Jaye. No one was in the store. He went back outside.

He saw Bert working on the hull of the big black ski boat. He had a mask over his nose and mouth. Jonah inched closer, stopping a little way back from the sleek craft. A heavy, chemical smell caught at the back of his throat.

"Don't worry, kid." Bert's voice was muffled under the mask. "Damage you done to the motor's all fixed."

Jonah let out his breath. He looked in the paper buckets at Bert's feet. They were filled with a clear goop that looked like rubber cement. Nearby were several small piles of white cloth. "You're patching the hole?" he asked.

Bert painted around the gash in the black hull with a brush. "Yup."

"Can I help?"

"Nope."

Jonah watched Bert put a thick circle of cloth over the center of the hole and a thinner but bigger circle over the first one. He painted over the circles with the goop. Working quickly, Bert continued to add circles of thin cloth, each slightly wider across than the last.

Bert brushed goop over each layer. He smoothed the edges until the hole was hidden by the last white circle. The patch was even with the outside of the hull.

"That's it?" Jonah blurted. "You fixed it with white cloth and rubber cement?"

Bert stepped away from the ski boat and removed his mask. It was the first time Jonah had seen him without a cigar. He looked at Jonah with one eyebrow raised. "Cloth an' rubber cement? This here's fiberglass an' resin." He patted his pockets and looked around. "Where's my stogie?"

Jonah followed Bert into the store. The old man pulled a new cigar from under the counter and lit it with his eyes closed. When he opened his eyes he hit a button on his cash register. The drawer opened with a loud *ka-ching*.

"Five hours, right?" Bert pulled bills from the register.

"There y'are, for your work on the moorin' floats." He handed twenty-five dollars across the counter to Jonah.

"But I still owe you the work on the Evinrude," Jonah said, confused.

"You're good for it," Bert grunted.

Jonah looked at the money in his hand. Twenty-five dollars more toward the Evinrude. And now he knew what to do about the hole in the skiff.

"How much does that patching stuff cost?" he asked.

"More'n what you got in your hand," Bert said.

More than twenty-five dollars? Jonah's hopes sank.

Bert chuckled in his silent way. "Rubber cement!" He shook his head.

Jonah slumped onto a stool.

Bert looked at him. "How big a hole you fixin' to work on?"

Jonah folded a five-dollar bill in half, and in half again. "Like that."

Bert puffed at his cigar. He blew smoke across Al and Lenny's empty stools. "I can't do much with that bit of left-overs down where I was workin'. I gotta sort it all out, but if you want it, you kin have it tomorrow."

"I can?" Jonah jumped up. "Thanks, Bert! I—"

"Don't you need to collect that sister of yours about now?" Bert scowled at him.

Jonah took one look at the clock and bolted for the door.

"An' watch you don't breathe the stuff," Bert called after him. "It'll make you dizzy in the head."

Jonah swerved up the lane to the dirt road. He now had seventy-nine dollars to put toward the Evinrude, more pay on the way from Sumi, and the materials he needed to patch his skiff.

You fix it, you bought it, Toolboy, Uncle Nate had said. Jonah would be careful about the fumes, all right. But his head was already spinning.

CHAPTER 18

Jonah was underwater. He could see the sun and the lit surface of the pond overhead. Shadows undulated below his kicking feet. He struggled up toward the light. A long tentacle brushed his leg and he shouted, bubbles rising from his open mouth. In the distance he heard the drone of an outboard motor. If he could just get to that boat, everything would be okay. He kicked harder and pulled himself through the water with his arms. The sound of the boat's motor grew louder. Its shadow passed overhead. From the darkness below, something wrapped itself around Jonah's ankle, pulling him down.

He woke up gasping for breath. His sheets were tangled around his legs. The hot water heater was chugging, and Jaye was snoring in her bunk above. Jonah lay on his back and waited for his heart to stop pounding.

His watch said six-thirty. He heard the back door slam and ducked out of bed. Uncle Nate was in the kitchen, rubbing his head with a towel.

"Morning, Toolboy," he said. "Rough night?"

"Huh?" Jonah rubbed the sleep from his eyes.

Uncle Nate put his arm around Jonah's shoulders and walked him over to the bathroom mirror. "I'm flattered and all," he said, "but, hey, get your own hairstyle."

Jonah laughed. His hair stuck up in as many directions as Uncle Nate's. "Bad dreams, I guess," he said. He sat at the counter and watched Uncle Nate put things into a backpack.

"Dreams are great stuff," Uncle Nate said. "Last night I dreamed the next scene in my novel. Of course, the star-crossed lovers were sea slugs." He waved his hand dismissively. "But *such romance!*" He zipped the pack and hefted it onto one shoulder. "Hey, I've got to head to the library early today. You don't mind being here on your own this morning, do you? I'm leaving you in charge."

"I'm definitely not in charge," Jonah said under his breath. He shook his head, thinking about the day before.

"Just tell her you're the boss," Uncle Nate said. "I said so."

Jonah jerked his head up in alarm. How did his uncle know about Sumi?

"Jayefish isn't giving you a hard time now, is she?" Uncle Nate looked at Jonah.

"What? Jaye? No," Jonah said quickly. "No trouble."

Uncle Nate picked up his bicycle helmet. "Okay, then. You sure you're all right?"

Jonah nodded. "I'm fine."

He followed Uncle Nate out the back door. Sparrows chased through the trees in the cool morning air.

"Maybe you're still a little shook up from your bad dream," Uncle Nate said. He straddled his rickety bicycle and mashed his hair under his helmet. "What was it about, anyway?"

Jonah glanced at the pond and shivered. "I forgot most of it already," he mumbled.

"Okay, Toolboy. Carry on, then, and have a great day. I'm off to kindle the romance!" Uncle Nate teetered away down the road. "On paper, of course."

Jonah smiled. A salty breeze blew in over the barrier beach. He felt glad that his uncle's writing was going so well. Things were looking up. His uncle had gone off to work inspired and happy. With Sumi's workboat fixed and ready to run, Jonah's own day had potential as well. The screen door creaked open.

"I'm coming with you today."

Jaye stood in the doorway in her nightgown.

"Jaye—" Jonah started.

"No." She set her jaw. "I thought it all out. You're taking me."

"I already told you. You wouldn't like it." He pushed past her and went into the kitchen. Jaye followed. "Besides," Jonah said, "you have to be at practice. Your team needs you."

"Yeah, right."

"You've got to be one of their best swimmers." Jonah looked at his sister. "Why don't you want to go today?"

"I don't know." She looked away.

Jonah took out bread for toast. Maybe she's still just homesick, he thought. But even so, she couldn't come to work with him. That would mess up everything.

"What's her name?" Jaye asked.

"Whose name?" Jonah pushed the toaster handle down.

"You know. That college girl you're working for."

"Oh. Sumi."

"That's a nice name," Jaye observed. "Is she nice?"

Jonah thought about the way Sumi checked her watch when he got to the marina. He thought about how she was always telling him what to do. "Not especially," he said.

"If she's not that nice, then why do you have to work for her?" Jaye lined up three or four boxes of cereal. She began creating a custom mixture. "Can't you just go out in Bert's boats?"

Jonah went to the picture window in the living room and looked out at the skiff. He grinned. If he got the patching stuff today from Bert, he could repair the hull over the weekend. Soon he would be finished fixing the Evinrude motor. His heart was beating fast. He turned to his sister.

"I'm going to have a boat of my own!"

Jaye's eyes grew wide. "You are?"

Then Jonah's whole plan spilled out, like a dam breaking. He told her how he was going to patch the skiff. How he was fixing the Evinrude for Bert. And how Sumi could pay him enough money to buy the motor for his own.

"Ten dollars an hour, Jaye! I'll take you out in my boat as much as you want. I promise. It's going to be so great!"

Jaye was quiet for a minute. "I guess so," she said. "I have to stay in shape for my real team at home, anyway." And she went into their room to get dressed.

Jonah felt as if a great burden had been lifted. He'd gotten so used to covering up his lies with more lies that he'd forgotten how much easier it was to tell the truth.

* * *

When Jonah got to the marina, Sumi glanced up from her chart and nodded. Instead of her usual cutoffs and a T-shirt, she was wearing a short wet suit. "Good," she said, "we can get started."

I guess I don't get extra credit for being early, Jonah thought.

"Let me tell you what we're doing today." She motioned for Jonah to join her at the chart. "First, you should know that I'm studying scallops."

Jonah already knew that from listening to Al and Lenny's complaints.

"I'm checking out the pond for prime scallop habitat— that means where they like to live best."

Did she teach nursery school in her spare time? "I know what habitat is," he muttered.

She ignored him and went on. "I've marked several places that should be good scallop habitat." She traced her finger over three separate sets of zigzagged lines on the chart. "One of these will be my study area. They're all pretty shallow, none more than six feet deep. Today we'll estimate how many adult scallops are in each area. Eventually we'll also be looking at coexistent species— plants and animals that live over the scallops in the water and in and on the salt pond bottom."

Jonah did not want to think about coexistent species. But he liked looking at the chart. It was like a diagram of the pond. At Sumi's instruction, he transferred a big plastic bin of gear—she called it the "lug"—from the van to the workboat.

"Those wet suit booties on top are for you," she told him.

"I've got my sneakers," Jonah said.

Sumi caught her hair and wound a hair band around it. "I wouldn't wear sneakers, but suit yourself," she said.

He shrugged. How wet was he going to get standing in a boat? Was she planning on capsizing?

Jonah tilted the motor off its lock and set the propeller in the water. Sumi put her chart under a Plexiglas lid on the console table. She tried to start the motor, but it wouldn't catch. Jonah adjusted the choke and the motor blared to life.

"I was going to do that," Sumi said. She started maneuvering the boat out of the marina. The engine coughed and ran low. Jonah readjusted the choke.

"Good," Sumi said.

When they got to the open pond, she increased their speed. Jonah hung onto the gunwale and leaned into the wind. He flexed his fingers, remembering the power in the Whaler's throttle the day before.

As they moved through the water, Sumi showed Jonah how to read the chart. She pointed out the coves by name and showed him how to recognize the shallows and hazards by the wavy concentric lines marking depth. He had to admit it *was* pretty interesting.

"We're getting near the first area," Sumi called over the motor's roar. She slowed the boat way down, and they rocked high on their own wake. She laughed. "I love that," she said.

Her laughter sounded different to Jonah when it wasn't at his expense. He looked across the pond toward the barrier beach. Churning water twisted through a cobble of sandbanks and disappeared into a pile of boulders at the shore.

"Ever been to the breachway?" Sumi asked, following his gaze.

Jonah wasn't sure what she was talking about.

"That's what you're looking at, isn't it?" She pointed to the boulders. "The breachway? The channel's marked by a rock wall on either side. It's tricky and rough in there, depending on the tide. Some fishing boats go out into the ocean through there, but not this one." She patted the workboat's gunwale. "I've been to the mouth of the breachway from the barrier beach, though." She shook her hair out of its band and pulled it back again into a sleek ponytail. "Even from there you can get washed off of the wall if you're not careful. People fishing from the rocks have drowned."

A cloud passed under the sun. The churning water of the breachway looked darker. Jonah checked the chart. One of the three sampling sites was on that side of the salt pond, but it wasn't very close to the breachway.

Jonah took over the console as they coasted into the first grid area. Sumi checked the temperature, current speed, and salinity at her sampling site and showed Jonah where to record them on her data sheets. Underneath the data sheets were enlargements of each of the areas.

"We're going to follow the grid lines and zigzag across the sample area. You want to go first?" Sumi asked.

"Okay," Jonah said.

She went to the stern and started sorting gear from the

lug. She pulled out a tow bar and fastened it to a clip on the winch. He nosed the workboat around toward where he thought the grid began.

"Here, you'd better suit up." She was holding out a wet suit.

Jonah let go of the wheel and backed away. Go first? She meant for him to get into the water? He felt his knees buckle.

The boat started spinning in a slow circle.

"The wheel!" Sumi pointed. "Don't let go!"

Jonah leaned forward and grabbed the steering wheel.

Sumi came up to the console table holding a mask, snorkel, and fins. "You should wait for me to take the wheel before you walk away," she chastised.

"You can go first," Jonah blurted. "You're all ready and everything, anyway."

"Okay, great!" Sumi said. She leaned over the gunwale and looked up at Jonah, her dark eyes flashing. "Really, I can't wait to go in. I was just being a polite host."

Jonah thought he might pass out with relief. He looked over the side of the boat at the water. Sun glinted off the surface. Dark shadows wavered below. No thanks, he thought.

Sumi sat on the wooden box and pulled on her fins. "When anyone goes in the water, the motor has to be in neutral or off. Today we'll put it in neutral. I'm going to hold the tow bar and drift back, and you can let out about twenty-five or thirty feet of cable. Then motor forward slowly and just follow along the grid lines. But watch me before you go. First I'll give you the diver's signal for okay." She patted her head. "You do it back to me. And don't wave. That means there's something wrong."

Jonah remembered how she had waved at him just before he'd grounded the Whaler. He felt his face grow red.

"I don't expect there'll be any problems...unless you drive over a sandbar."

Jonah was sure he saw her crack a smile as she adjusted her mask. He blew out a long breath.

"When I hold up two fingers," Sumi continued, "write a two at that spot on the grid sheet. When I hold up one finger, write a one. If I hold up a closed fist—"

"I'll write 'scallop power,'" Jonah said under his breath.

Sumi smiled. "That's actually funny," she said. "But write in a zero. Okay, I'm going in."

Jonah pulled the throttle back to neutral. Sumi slipped over the side. She flashed him a grin just before she put the snorkel in her mouth. Jonah flipped the switch on the winch and let the cable play out. He watched Sumi drop back away from the boat. When she was out about twenty-five feet, he stopped the winch. He could see her pat her head with her hand. He felt a little goofy, but he returned the signal. Then he pushed the throttle forward.

It was a challenge for Jonah to follow the grid and record Sumi's signals at the same time. He was pleased with the system he devised, mastering the rhythm of boat and pond. I am a boat guy, he thought. I am *the* boat guy.

Jonah needn't have worried that Sumi would want to swap jobs. When she finished the first grid and signaled to switch, her okay came back almost before Jonah had finished his thumb's down for no. She even rode the tow bar on the way to the two other grid areas.

"Sorry to have hogged all the fun," Sumi said after she'd climbed aboard and pulled off her mask. "It's just so amazing down there. That one scallop bed—it's phenomenal! Loads of adult scallops. Eelgrass everywhere. Pipefish darting around like kids playing hide and seek. And the most beautiful, iridescent ctenophores!"

"Teena-fours?" Jonah repeated.

"It's a kind of jellyfish," Sumi said.

Jonah felt a chill down his back. His leg began to throb and burn. He didn't care how much fun she said it was. He was never getting in that water. Not ever.

CHAPTER 19

Saturday morning Jonah set his repair materials on the kitchen counter. First the big metal can of resin. Then the smaller one to mix with it. He laid out the scraps of fiberglass cloth, some thick, some thin, and some banded together and labeled "Woven Roving."

"Woven roving," Jonah said. "Woven roving woven woving roven woving." He laughed out loud. Good thing Uncle Nate and Jaye aren't here listening to me, he decided. They already think I'm crazy to stay home and work on a boat instead of spending the day at the beach with them.

Bert had given Jonah paper buckets that looked like Chinese takeout containers, as well as sandpaper, gloves, a couple of disposable brushes, and a mask. These aren't leftovers, Jonah thought. Most of this stuff has never been used. He pictured Bert's frown as he'd handed over the bag. That old guy's grouch act had a few holes of its own.

Jonah read the instructions on the backs of the resin cans. He tried to remember everything Bert had done to fix the hole in the black ski boat. Then Jonah lined up his materials on the counter, switching places until they were in order for what he had to do to patch his skiff.

Taking only the sandpaper with him, he went outside. He slid the skiff, already right side up, into the shade of the trees at the edge of the sandy beach. He ran his hand along the shreds of fiberglass fringing the hole. When he rubbed the sandpaper over one edge, white dust rose into the air. He went back in to get the gloves and the mask.

As he sanded, he wished for even the slightest hint of a breeze. The sun inched its way overhead and beyond. Sweat trickled down his back. Finally he took off one glove and ran his finger over the gash in the hull. The edges were smooth and tapered into the intact fiberglass of the hull. It was ready.

Jonah went back inside and rummaged in Uncle Nate's kitchen drawers until he found a pair of scissors. First he cut a piece of the fiberglass cloth into the shape of the hole, just big enough to overlap the edges of the center of the gash. Then he cut more pieces, making each one just a tiny bit bigger around than the one before it. He took everything out to the waiting boat and set up his materials on an old board.

"Roven woving weady," he said, grinning under the mask.

He took a deep breath and flexed his fingers. Once he mixed the resins in the paper bucket, he knew he'd have to work quickly. The directions said the resin would set up in as little as twenty minutes.

The heavy smell wreathed up his nose as soon as he opened the cans. Jonah grimaced as he mixed the resins. He painted resin around the gash and applied the smallest patch of fiberglass cloth to the hull. Then he added the next bigger piece and the next, painting each layer with resin.

He alternated working the inside and outside of the hull. He had to trim some of the fiberglass shapes as he worked, even after they'd been soaked with resin. Uncle Nate's scissors acquired a hairy mat of fibers along the blades.

And then just like that, it was done. Jonah sat back and watched his repair solidify into a translucent, yellowy patch. He touched it with the sticky gloves, then felt the solid resin and fiberglass with his bare fingers. It was dry.

He put his foot on the gunwale. "Boat guy," he nodded.

Jonah stuffed the empty cans and paper buckets into the trash, slipping in Uncle Nate's ruined scissors. He'd buy a new pair from Bert's store before his uncle even noticed. Too bad. That would probably set him back about five dollars.

Jonah took a bucket of water and a scrub brush and cleaned the skiff inside and out. He found the piece of rope Uncle Nate had used for his shoddy table repair and cut it in two. Then Jonah slid the skiff into the water and tied both the bow and stern to the dock. Climbing in, he lay back in his boat and folded his hands behind his head. He closed his eyes and sighed.

* * *

Jonah felt a shadow come between him and the sun and opened his eyes. He saw a tall, thin silhouette with a halo of wild hair. He heard the outdoor shower running next to the cabin.

"Pretty resourceful, aren't you, Toolboy?" Uncle Nate said. He bent to run his hand over the inside patch. "I won't even ask how you figured this one out. I'm truly impressed, but then again, you always have that effect on me." He put his hand on Jonah's shoulder. Jonah looked down, his throat suddenly tight.

The sun was low in the sky, and a stiff offshore wind was kicking up. The skiff thudded against the dock, beating time to the choppy waves.

"I think there's something down here that can help." Uncle Nate reached into the water next to the dock and felt around one of the wooden pilings. "Aha!" he said, pulling on a rope. At its end was an algae-covered float. Uncle Nate grinned from ear to ear. He yanked another from under the next piling, holding it up like a prize.

"Thanks." Jonah winced at the grimy floats. "Thanks a lot."

"Okeydokey then," Uncle Nate said. "I'll hunt around for some oars later. Right now I'd better go and start the grill." He walked toward the deck, then stopped. "Listen, as far as boating safety rules go, you have to have a life vest—that's the law. I think there's an old one under the deck. Next, I always have to be here and know when you're going out. And the last rule is stay away from the breachway. It's too rough in there—even the pros have trouble. Got it?"

Jonah nodded. He found a scraper under the deck near the life vest. The gunky green floats smelled worse than the resin. Scrape the floats, scrape the floats—this could give you some kind of nightmares, he thought. He looked up at his skiff rocking on the waves and smiled.

"Wow, Jonah!" Jaye joined him at the water's edge, bringing the welcome smell of clean skin and newly washed hair. "The boat really works. It's floating!"

"That's what boats do," Jonah said. He flicked a blob of muck off of his arm.

"Can I get in it?" She walked out onto the dock.

"Wait." Jonah tied the clean floats to the pilings. The skiff bumped against them with muffled taps.

"Can I get in now?" Jaye was already stepping aboard.

A sudden selfishness overtook Jonah. He wanted to tell her to get out. "Take off your shoes," he said instead.

"When are you going to take me for a ride?" Jaye demanded. "You promised."

"I don't have the motor," he reminded her. "I can't even take it out myself yet."

"But you said you would." Jaye crossed her arms.

"Jaye—"

"Hey, you two goofballs!" Uncle Nate came out on the back deck. He was holding the grill rack. A long piece of aluminum foil fluttered out from his hands like a banner. "I want to trim this so it's round. Anybody seen the kitchen scissors?"

* * *

Uncle Nate yawned. "Well, it's Sunday night already," he said, stretching his long arms. "Tomorrow's another work week."

"Tomorrow's not a week," Jaye said. "It's a day."

"Didn't know you were such a stickler for words, Jayefish." Uncle Nate poked her in the ribs. "How about a walk on the beach to cap off the night?"

"Kind of dark for that, isn't it?" Jonah said.

Uncle Nate put his hand on his heart. "Look at that full moon. Ever been on the beach under a full moon?"

"I bet it's romantic," Jaye sighed.

"That's it." Uncle Nate jumped up. "I must go in the name of research. You two can be my assistants. To the bicycles, research assistants!"

The moon lit the deserted road in a soft blue glow. They rode in the opposite direction from Bert's store and the town beach, toward the barrier beach. When they crested the dune path, the ocean spread out below them in shimmering motion.

Silently they lay their bikes down on the path. Jonah took off his shoes and let the cooling sand slip between his toes. He crossed the beach to the lifeguard chair and climbed to the top. As he looked out over the ocean, the swells rose and fell in time with his own breathing.

Jaye climbed up into the chair next to him. He felt her hand slip into his and he let her hold on. They tucked up their legs and sat listening to the waves break and recede, break and recede on the glistening shore. Uncle Nate walked along the water's edge, staring out to sea.

Other voices drifted toward them from the bicycle path.

"Come on," Jonah heard someone say, and then "Wait for me!" Running steps in the sand stopped at the foot of the lifeguard chair.

"Someone's already up there," a girl's voice whispered.

"Who cares?" a boy answered. "Let's go up."

"Wait," another girl whined.

Jonah felt the chair shake and in another second three kids' faces rose above the edge of the seat. One of them looked like the big kid from Jaye's swim team.

"Who are you?" a little girl asked.

"Who are *you?*" Jonah teased. He could feel Jaye gripping his hand.

"Oooh look, it's KJ," the boy said. "Little Kiddie lose her bottle?"

"What's your major problem?" Jonah demanded.

"Calling all research assistants!" Uncle Nate imitated a loudspeaker, his voice booming over the sound of the waves.

The three intruders jumped off the chair rungs and scattered.

Jonah helped Jaye climb down. "That kid's just stupid," he told her.

"He's mean. He knows I'm not twelve. He says I better not beat him in the time trials anymore."

"Are they all like that?" Jonah asked.

She didn't answer.

"Want me to beat them up for you?" he offered. It was their standing joke.

Jaye didn't laugh. "I want to quit," she said. "I want to go out in a boat every day, like you."

"I'll take you out," he told her. "I promised that I would, and I will."

"Tomorrow?"

"I have to work tomorrow, Jaye, so I can get money to buy the motor."

"So you just made that up about taking me in a boat. If you're so good at telling stories, then why can't you finish seventh-grade English?"

Jaye turned and trudged to where Uncle Nate was waiting on the bike path. Jonah hurried after her. She got on her bike without a word. The crunch of their tires on dirt and stones ripped through the tense silence of the ride back.

CHAPTER 20

On Monday, Jonah was already on the workboat when Sumi drove up in her van. He had filled the boat's outboard tank with gas and was pulling the motor back off its tilt lock, using his body as a counterweight.

Sumi climbed aboard. She stuck the key in the ignition and slipped her chart under its Plexiglas cover on the console table. "Here." She tapped on the Plexiglas with her finger.

Jonah released the prop down into the water and joined her at the console.

"I analyzed our data from Friday, and this is going to be my study site." Sumi pointed at a mark on the map. It was the site across the pond nearest the barrier beach. Jonah remembered her signals there, her thin arm shooting up out of the water—two fingers, two fingers, and two fingers again. Loaded with scallops, she'd said.

She hopped up onto the dock and went back to the van. The big plastic lug full of equipment slid from the van to the ground with a crash. Jonah hurried over to grab the other handle.

"Quadrat sampling today," she said as they hoisted the lug into the workboat.

Jonah didn't have a clue what she meant. She flipped through her data sheets, making notes. He stood at the stern with one hand on the motor. He looked over his shoulder at the general store and then out to the pond, shifting from foot to foot. Sumi continued to work.

Jonah cleared his throat. He took a deep breath. "Want me to take us out?" he asked in what he hoped was his most casual-sounding voice.

Sumi shook her head, no. "I'll do it as soon as—" She glanced up at him and stopped. "Sure," she said, sitting down on the wooden storage box. "Go ahead."

"Right." Jonah turned to untie the lines.

Jonah started up the motor, then nosed the workboat through the marina. He drove through the cove with only the smallest wake, careful not to come too close to any of the other boats. When he got out into the open salt pond, he eased the throttle forward as far as it would go. The bow lifted into the air and the workboat shot across the pond. The wind roared in his ears. Jonah felt pure momentum channel up his arm and into his body from the boat's throttle. He was speed. He was power.

"Where's the fire?" Sumi yelled in his ear. She smiled and clutched her clipboard against her with one hand, trying to rein in her hair with the other. She closed her eyes and leaned into the wind.

As they approached the study site he cut back the throttle, letting the boat ride up on its wake. Sumi looked over and laughed.

Why didn't I ever think of being a marine biologist?
Jonah wondered. This is a great job. Noticing that the
water was getting shallow, he pulled the throttle back to
neutral, cut the motor, and tilted out the prop.

"Ready to go in?" Sumi asked. She held out the extra
pair of wet suit booties. "It's pretty shallow, but sneakers
won't cut it today."

Right, Jonah thought. This is the reason I'll never be a
marine biologist. "I'll just drive the boat, I guess," he told
her.

"Drive where?" She gave him a quizzical look. "This is
it." She put down the booties and tossed the anchor over
the side. "We're here. I've got the site divided into three
sections. In each place we're going to drop this half-meter
quadrat." She held up a square metal frame with a small
float attached to it. "We dig down into the sand inside the
square about two inches, and we dump the sand we dig up
into this," she said, grabbing a big bucket. "Then we sieve
through it to identify other species."

"Shouldn't I stay here and write down what you find?"
Jonah offered.

"We'll bring waterproof paper and a wax pencil," Sumi
said. She took the metal square and stepped off the back of
the boat. "Why don't you grab the pail and shovels?" She
consulted her clipboard and waded away from the boat.

Jonah gulped. He put a shovel inside the pail and
leaned over the gunwale. He saw Sumi close her eyes and
toss the square over her shoulder. It splashed into the
water and sank to the bottom. The little float bobbed on
the surface.

Jonah waved the pail and shovel at Sumi. "Here," he called.

She waded back and stood below Jonah. "What's with you and the water? Wait a minute!" Her eyes narrowed slightly. "Can't you swim?" She folded her arms. "You have no business taking this job if you can't—"

"I can swim." Jonah was indignant. "I'm in lifesaving class."

"Really?" She looked at him with interest. "How do you do that without getting in the water?"

"I go in water," he said through clenched teeth. "Pool water."

"But the salt pond is so much better than a pool!" Sumi said. She splashed her hands around her.

He knew she would laugh at him. How could he admit to her that he was afraid? "Not to me," he mumbled.

"This is beautiful, clean ocean water," she insisted, her voice rising. "It washes in twice a day through the breachway. How could anyone not like swimming in the ocean?"

"I just don't want to come in, okay?" Jonah burst out. His voice sounded strange in his own ears, loud and a lot higher than normal.

He turned from her, shaking. He couldn't make himself get in the water. He just couldn't. This is it, he thought. My new job is over. Jonah knew that if he didn't work for Sumi, he'd never earn enough money to buy the Evinrude. Why did he have to get stung by that stupid man-of-war? Now all of his plans were ruined.

The workboat rocked as Sumi climbed aboard. He heard her shifting gear around the deck. He didn't move.

She'd probably just drive them back to the marina. Then he'd get off the boat and ride away on his bike. He would not come back to work for her. And there would be no point in coming back to Bert's. He heard her come near and held his breath. He wished he were back home in the city or anywhere else.

"On second thought," Sumi said, "I think you're right. The data sheets will get too messed up in the water. One of us had better dig and sieve, and the other one should sort and record here at the worktable. How are you at identifying things from diagrams?"

Jonah turned and leaned against the gunwale. He breathed slowly, trying to calm down. Maybe she hadn't even noticed how upset he was. He hoped she hadn't.

Sumi flipped to a set of plastic laminated sketches of clams and snails on the clipboard and held it out. Jonah took it from her. The line drawings had lots of details having to do with shape, color, and size. It seemed like a schematic, only of marine animals instead of spark plugs and wiring. He coughed, trying to get rid of the tightness in his throat. "I'm pretty okay at diagrams." His voice sounded thick in his ears.

"Great," Sumi said. "This will work out really well." She handed him a pair of gloves. Then she went back into the water.

* * *

"That's the last of it," Sumi said, wiping her face on her sleeve. Jonah leaned over the side and poured water from the bucket through the muddy sand on her sieve. The sand melted away, revealing two scallops, five small clams, three snails, a hermit crab, and something that looked like a thumb made out of lead.

"Look at that," Sumi said. She picked up the lead figure. "It's a toy soldier—a really old one!"

She handed him the soldier and the sieve and pulled herself onto the workboat.

Jonah turned the lead soldier over in his hand, feeling the weight of it. "Buried treasure," he said. He wedged the figure in between a couple of boards in the bow.

Sumi smiled. "He will be our mascot," she said. "Our hero."

She looked over Jonah's shoulder as he sorted the contents of the sieve into various piles. He compared two fingernail-sized clams to one of the sketches.

"I don't expect you to be able to tell the difference between those clams," she said.

Jonah placed each of the small bivalves in a different pile. "I can do it," he said.

She examined his work. He saw her smile just a little. "Finished the counts?" she asked.

Jonah handed her the completed data sheets and lifted the outer side of the worktable box. He emptied the bucket onto the tilted worktable, letting the water carry his creatures—lavender, pink, and amber like a handful of polished stones—over the side and back to their home in the pond. It hadn't been so bad having the sea animals up close where he could get a good look at them. Now he watched them drift through the shallow water. The clams dug in as soon as they came to rest on the sand. The hermit crabs scuttled away into the shadows.

Sumi leaned into the wooden box to stow the clipboard and her other gear, coming up with a small cooler. She gave Jonah a cold bottle of water and twisted the cap off of her own.

"Thanks," Jonah said. He held the plastic bottle up to his forehead.

"And here's a bonus." She passed him a giant chocolate chip cookie and watched his face as he bit into it. "It's great, right?"

He nodded, chewing.

"My mom's special cookies, direct from California." Sumi leaned back against the gunwale and closed her eyes.

Jonah hadn't even thought about her having parents, or about her being from somewhere else. California was a long way from here.

"Do you miss home?" he asked.

"I'm at home anywhere, as long as I can get in the water," Sumi said. She didn't open her eyes. Her face was tipped toward the sun and her skin glowed the color of coffee ice cream. One of her eyebrows arched sharply, he noticed. The other was a smooth curve. There was a faint crust of dried salt on her cheek.

"Well," she said, opening one eye and squinting at him. "We'd better head in."

She stood in the bow as Jonah drove the workboat slowly back across the pond. The sun caught tips of waves, making them sparkle like liquid diamonds. He mulled over Sumi's words. She spent every moment she could in the water, and nothing bad had happened to her. She was okay. She was fine.

In fact, Jonah thought, she was just about perfect.

* * *

Someone was standing on the end of the dock as they approached the marina. As they chugged in closer, Jonah could see it was a small someone. Someone in a bathing suit with two dark braids. What was Jaye doing there?

"Hi!" Jaye waved. She ran along the dock, following the workboat as Jonah edged it into its slip.

"Hello." Sumi looked from Jaye to Jonah, smiling.

"My sister," Jonah muttered. He glared at Jaye, then busied himself tying up the boat.

"I'm Jaye," his sister said. "You're Sumi, right?"

Jonah felt his face and ears burn.

"Nice to meet you, Jaye." Sumi reached up to shake hands.

Sumi hoisted the lug up onto the dock and climbed out of the boat. Jonah started to follow her, but Jaye grabbed the other side of the lug and walked Sumi to the van.

"What did you guys do today? Did you go in the water? Was it fun?" Jaye chattered to Sumi the whole way.

He watched them open the van and load the gear together. I should be doing that, he thought. He tilted out the propeller and grabbed the boat key.

At the van, he handed the key to Sumi. "We have to go."

"No we don't," Jaye said. "We still have—"

"We're late," Jonah interrupted. He got Jaye's bike and leaned it against her so she had to take it. Then he got his own.

"Tomorrow we won't be going out on the pond," Sumi

told Jonah. "We'll be putting together a scallop collector—working here." She opened the driver's side door of the van. "I have to get my materials together. I probably won't be down until three or so." She reached up and let her hair fall from its knot. Jonah watched it swing down in a shiny black curtain. She climbed in the van and drove off.

Jonah noticed Jaye watching him. Her face wore an odd little smile.

"What are you doing here?" he demanded.

"I wanted to see all the fun you're having," she told him.

"It's not that much fun," he said. "See? Tomorrow I'm not even going out on the pond."

"Umm-hmm." Jaye nodded, still smiling.

"I'm just going to be working here. Boring stuff. Fixing equipment."

Jaye got on her bicycle and started up the lane.

Jonah pedaled after her. Had she skipped out of swim team early? He felt a rising panic. Had she stayed there at all? Jonah caught up even with Jaye. He saw that her braids were wet. She had the telltale goggle marks near her eyes.

"You're not even supposed to be here," he huffed. "You have to wait for me at the town beach."

"I can ride by myself," Jaye said. "I don't need you. And don't tell me what to do."

Jonah didn't like the sound of that.

CHAPTER 21

Jaye went to swim team practice the next day without a protest. Surprised, Jonah kept his mouth shut. But he couldn't shake the feeling that his sister might show up at the marina again anytime.

Bert was alone when Jonah entered the store. "Where's your boss?" Bert asked.

"She's coming later, around three. She's up at the college getting our materials."

"Guess you kin get back to work on *our* Evinrude," Bert said. His mouth curled in a grin around his cigar.

"Yeah, I will." Jonah ducked out back. He wondered exactly what Bert thought was so funny.

The Evinrude was waiting right where he'd left it on the stand in the lean-to. He took a moment to add up the hours he'd worked for Sumi. Together with what he'd already saved, he had over a hundred and fifty dollars. Jonah ran his hand along the motor's cover, then leaned over and wrapped his arms around it. You're going to be mine, he thought. Mine.

Taking the cover off, he checked the work he'd already done on the head of the motor. It was in pretty good shape. He spread the schematic on the workbench and studied it. Then he went back to the Evinrude and unbolted the case to the lower unit. The propeller, attached to a long, upright drive-shaft, slid down from the engine and into his hands.

Jonah held up the lower unit so he could inspect the prop. It wasn't bent. It just needed a scrubbing to get the barnacles off.

He clamped the lower unit to the workbench and removed the housing screws and washers. The housing wouldn't budge, so he gave it a tap with a rubber mallet to loosen it. It slid up and off the gear shaft. Inside was the impeller, shaped like a paddle wheel. Jonah knew that the little wheel pushed water around inside the motor to cool it. He picked it up and checked it carefully. It was cracked in a few places. He pried off all of the rubber O-rings and gaskets that kept the connections watertight. Old and worn, thought Jonah. He gathered up the O-rings and the impeller and headed inside.

"S'pose you'll be wantin' new ones," Bert said. He squinted at Jonah's collection of motor parts and disap-peared into the stockroom. Jonah sat down on a stool and spun around in circles. With the TV off, the tinny radio and the whir of Bert's fan seemed almost like quiet. Jonah drank in the smell of oil on his hands. He put his forehead down on the counter and swung his stool from side to side.

"That some new kinda exercise?" Bert asked. He dumped a handful of parts on the counter next to Jonah's head and set a tube of oil next to the new impeller. "Don't forget to drain the oil and grease it up when you put it back together."

"Thanks." Jonah held out the bottom of his shirt and

swept the pile of parts into it. He went back out to the lean-to and spilled the parts onto the workbench.

Nothing captivated Jonah like setting all of those clean, new parts into the Evinrude one by one. The only thing that even came close was driving the Whaler full-throttle. He drained foul-smelling oil out of the lower unit and replaced it with the contents of Bert's tube, making sure there were no air bubbles inside. Then he greased the driveshaft and reassembled the motor. He took a step back from the Evinrude and looked it over.

"Where'd you learn how to fix a motor like that?" Sumi was standing at the side of the lean-to, watching him.

Jonah's heartbeat quickened. "Around," he said. He turned away from her and grabbed the motor's cover, hugging it to his chest.

Wait until it's on my skiff, he thought, grinning. Just wait until you see that.

* * *

After he'd put the cover back on the Evinrude, Jonah went with Sumi to unload her van.

"Hey, airhead! Joining with the forces of doom?" Al slammed the door of his truck. Lenny chuckled, following his father into Bert's store.

Sumi set the ropes, buoys, and nets she was carrying on the ground. "Why does he call you airhead?" she asked Jonah.

"Why does he call you forces of doom?"

Sumi pursed her lips. "I think he's joking. But Al's worried about scallop fishing this fall." She glanced at the store. "There was a bad brown algae bloom last year that killed lots of scallops. There won't be many adult scallops for harvest this year, and since those are the ones that reproduce, there won't be many to replace them next year, either."

"What's that got to do with you?" Jonah asked.

"Nothing, really." Sumi shrugged. "What I'm doing could actually help the scallops, but these guys think I'm just 'messing with things.'" She looked across the pond toward her study site. "Scallops start out as tiny, swimming larvae—babies, that is. When they grow to a certain size, they grab onto something near the bottom, like eelgrass, or another shell, and start to grow." She held up a roll of netting and a big mesh bag like the kind onions come in. "I'm going to give them extra places to grab onto. I think it will help protect the scallops—spat, they're called when they settle down—and increase the population."

Sumi's dark eyes glittered. She had been waving her hands around as she spoke. She looked so charged up that Jonah didn't even mind that she'd called the larvae "babies" for his benefit.

She turned to Jonah. "Sound like 'forces of doom' to you?" She let out a thin laugh.

Jonah shook his head.

"Well, I don't know if it'll work," Sumi said, "but I do know one thing. You're no airhead." She laughed again in a way that made Jonah smile down to his toes.

Sumi showed him how to stuff pieces of netting into the onion bags. When the bags were full, they clipped them along three ropes. She explained that they would rig the ropes with floats at the top and weights at the bottom so the bags would hang suspended in the water. Jonah loaded three cement sinkers into the work skiff and stowed the ropes and bags in the built-in wooden box. Sumi rocked on the balls of her feet.

"I planned this all of last semester, and now I finally get to try it out," she said.

Jonah thought about his skiff and the Evinrude, repaired and ready to try, and he knew just how Sumi felt. Helping her was turning out to be the best thing he'd ever done, for all kinds of reasons. He stepped up onto the dock. She reached up and he took her hand, pulling her onto the dock next to him.

"I can't wait for tomorrow!" she exclaimed.

Footsteps rang out at the shore end of the aluminum dock.

"What's happening tomorrow?" Jaye said.

Jonah looked at his watch in alarm. It was after five.

"We're going out in the boat to set up my scallop collectors," Sumi told Jaye. She gave one of Jaye's wet braids a tug.

Jonah tensed.

"Great," Jaye said. "Did Jonah tell you? I'm coming, too."

"What?" Jonah said.

"I have to have something to do now that swim team is over for me."

"What are you talking about?" Swim team isn't over, Jonah thought.

Jaye faced him. He thought he saw her lower lip quiver.

"If I can't come with *you*," she said, "then I'd better ask *Uncle Nate* what I should do."

"Of course you can come," Sumi said.

Jonah just stood there with his mouth open.

CHAPTER 22

I don't care if you won't talk to me," Jaye told Jonah the next afternoon. She tossed her braids and leaned her bicycle against a tree near the general store. "Why should I be on a swim team with mean kids who don't want me to swim fast?"

Because the swim team is somewhere else, Jonah thought. He watched Sumi carry a gas can to the workboat. She was wearing her wet suit, ready to go in the water again.

"She goin' out?" Bert motioned at Jaye with his cigar.

"Yes." Jonah cringed inside.

"She's gotta wear a vest," Bert said.

Jaye was indignant. "I'm a champion swi—"

"Don't matter if you're a Navy SEAL. Everyone's gotta *have* a vest. Under twelve and you gotta *wear* one." He reached behind the soda machine, tossed an ancient orange life vest at Jonah, and went inside.

Jonah stared at the spot where the old man had been. He should tell Bert that the Evinrude was fixed. But what if someone else bought it before he earned the rest of the money?

"Ready?" Sumi called.

Jaye ran down the dock and jumped into the boat. "Ready!"

Jonah followed. He tossed the vest to Jaye.

"I'm not wearing this," she said.

The screen door of the store creaked. Bert glowered in the doorway, his arms folded across his chest.

Jaye pulled the bulky horseshoe-shaped vest over her head and tied it in front. "I bet I swim better than him," she grumbled.

"This is it," Sumi said. She went to the bow and saluted the lead soldier. She smiled at Jonah. "Okay, take us out, cap'n!" She saluted him, too.

Jonah was glad to turn and drop the prop into the water so he could hide his goofy grin. He started the motor and headed out of the cove toward Sumi's study site. Their study site. A few mountainous white clouds lazed across the sky.

"What are you smiling about?" Jaye yelled to him above the motor's roar.

Jonah glanced at Sumi. She sat on the wooden box with her legs tucked, facing out over the bow.

He glared at his sister. "I like to drive the boat, okay?"

She rolled her eyes.

"How about a swim?" Jonah said. He pushed Jaye against the gunwale with his hip.

"Hey!" she yelled.

Jonah stepped back, aware of Sumi's eyes on him. Jaye was making him act like a kid. She was already ruining everything.

When they got to the study site, he cut the motor and set the anchor. Far off at the town beach, Jonah heard whistles. He squinted. It seemed like a lot more activity than usual over there. A few small boats motored far across the pond.

Sumi checked the water temperature, salinity, and current speed. Jonah tripped over his sneaker lace hurrying to get the clipboard.

"When are we going in the water?" Jaye asked. She tugged at the vest.

"You like to swim?" Sumi asked Jaye.

Great, Jonah said to himself. Here we go.

Jaye launched into an epic about her swim team back home, her events, her medals, blah, blah, blah. Like a yapping puppy, Jonah thought, watching her follow Sumi around the deck.

While Jaye chatted, Jonah worked with Sumi setting up the scallop spat collectors. They attached cement sinkers to the ends of the ropes and checked the bags and floats. One of the onion bags came off its rope.

Sumi shook her head. "I must have used a broken ring yesterday. I know you wouldn't have let that go by," she said to Jonah. She replaced the ring.

Jonah was standing next to Jaye. He stood straighter and pulled his shoulders back.

"Hey, Sumi, what's this?" Jaye swung her hand toward the wooden pulley on the end of the davit, but missed it.

Jonah reached up and held onto the pulley. "That's what we use to set out and pull in equipment," he told her, using his deepest voice.

Jaye ignored him. "Are we going in the water?" she asked Sumi.

"Well," Sumi said, "I'd like to set out the collectors from here in the boat. I think we'll get it done pretty quickly. Then I challenge you to a race."

"You're on!" Jaye clapped her hands.

Jonah gave his sister a withering look. She didn't seem to notice.

"Let's get started," Sumi said. She hauled in the anchor while Jonah started up the motor.

It was difficult work maneuvering the boat to set the sinkers where Sumi wanted them. A couple of times Jonah had to hoist the motor partway out of the water, straining against its weight to keep the propeller off the sandy bottom.

When the three collector lines were set, Sumi checked the current speed again. "Tide's going out pretty fast now," she said. They watched the top onion bags float out horizontal on the surface, pulled by the moving water.

"Shoot," Sumi banged her fist into her hand. "I needed to weight the bags."

"Do we have to pull them all back in again?" Jaye whined. She was leaning over the gunwale, trailing her fingers in the water.

Sumi rummaged in the wooden box and brought out a bag of lead sinkers. "I think I can fix these in the water," she said. "It shouldn't take me too long."

Jonah turned off the motor and set the anchor again.

"I'll help," Jaye said. She jumped over the side with a splash.

Sumi clipped the bag of sinkers to her waist with a rope and plunged in. The water was almost up to her shoulders. As she neared the first collector line, a couple of bags came loose and floated away in the current.

"Oh no!" Sumi cried. She swam away to retrieve the bags.

Jonah watched from the boat as more and more of the bags came loose. Jaye darted around grabbing at them. Jonah thought he should be the one helping Sumi, not Jaye.

I'm going in, he decided. He put his foot over the gunwale and looked into the water. The biggest crab he'd ever seen swam by sideways near the surface. Below, the water was murky and full of dark shadows. Jonah pulled his foot back. He couldn't do it.

Instead, he hooked some of the bags with a pole and dragged them into the boat.

"That was fun!" Jaye exclaimed. She tossed her armload of bags at Jonah. Seaweed slapped his arm and he batted it away.

"It's a good thing you're such a strong swimmer, Jaye," Sumi said.

Jonah slumped against the console table.

"I think that's all of them." Sumi tossed onion bags ahead of her and climbed into the boat. "We'll have to pull the lines in and start again." She looked grim.

"This stupid thing is bothering me," Jaye complained. She was floating in the water, only her eyes visible above the orange vest. "It keeps pushing up in front of my face."

"Under twelve, you've got to wear it," Jonah said.

"Like you're so much older," Jaye said.

Jonah glanced at Sumi. She was busy with the bags.

Jaye climbed back into the boat so they could motor around and pick up the three spat collector lines. Her lips looked purple from being in the cool water so long. They anchored again to make repairs. Jonah sat down with one of the onion bags and took out a new plastic ring. When he removed the old ring from the top of the bag, he saw that the plastic had been sliced apart with something sharp. He sucked in a breath.

Sumi was leaning over his shoulder. "I know," she said quietly. "It looks like it was cut on purpose."

* * *

Jaye sulked on the way back to the marina. Resetting the collectors had taken the rest of the afternoon, and there had been no time for swim races or anything else. Sumi was very quiet. Jonah saw her shiver a bit in the wind. She drove the boat slowly, staring straight ahead, her jaw set.

They tied the boat up at the dock. Jaye jumped off and tossed the orange vest on the beach. She flopped in the sun near her bicycle.

"I guess I'm going to have to keep a better eye on things," Sumi told Jonah. She climbed into her van and rolled down the window.

"I think I can see the study site from my uncle's," Jonah said. "I'll help you watch."

She looked down at him. "Thanks. You're really great,"

she said. She smiled. "But listen." She ducked down and came up with a scrap of paper and a pencil. "Here's my number. If you see anything weird, don't go out there by yourself. Just call me, okay?"

Jonah took the paper. "Okay," he said. He folded it again and again and put the tiny square in his pocket. He kept his hand on it. When Sumi drove away, Jaye was watching him.

Having Jaye here spoils everything, Jonah thought. She made him look stupid for staying in the boat. He should have just told Sumi the truth about the Portuguese man-of-war in the first place. Now it was too late. And Jaye would show him up every afternoon—unless he told Uncle Nate about Mr. Ritchie's letter himself.

"Uncle Nate," he could say, "I want to fill you in on all of the big fat lies I've been telling you since we got here."

Jonah shook his head. If only he hadn't started with the lies at all. Now he felt trapped. He kicked a rock down the beach. It skipped off of Jaye's life vest. He walked down, grabbed the vest, and went to put it behind Bert's soda machine. Through the screen door he saw Lenny and Al.

"Hey, airhead!" Al yelled. "I think you and that girl left some trash out on the pond."

Jonah stopped. Was Al talking about setting out the spat collectors? Or did he know something about those cut rings? Frowning, Jonah put the life vest away.

Bert came out of the store. His cigar bobbed up and down. "How'd your patch job turn out?" he asked.

"Huh? Oh, good," Jonah said. He pictured his skiff, waiting at Uncle Nate's dock.

"She in the water?"

Jonah nodded. "Over there." He motioned to the north-east side of the salt pond.

"Better bring her 'round," Bert squinted. "We kin test out that Evinrude on Saturday."

"On my skiff?" Jonah burst out. "Put the Evinrude on my skiff?"

"Gotta make sure it's really workin' an' not just lookin' good." Bert squinted even harder.

Jonah gave a little jump in the air. "All right!" he told Bert. "I'll..." His voice trailed off. "...I can't get her here," he finished.

"Whyn't you row her over?" Bert suggested.

"No oars."

"I got some you kin take."

Jonah followed Bert around back. They shifted through a pile of old oars for a usable pair.

"Jonah!" Jaye was calling him.

He thanked Bert over and over. The old man waved him away. Jonah balanced the oars across his handlebars and teetered back to the cabin. He would tell Uncle Nate that a friend gave him the oars, which, odd as it was, seemed true.

* * *

"I know I don't usually work evenings," Uncle Nate said after dinner. "But can you two manage if I disappear again just this once? My book is cookin'!" He dipped a ladle into a big pot and scraped out the last of the chili. "Now my characters are really falling in love." He waved the ladle, dripping gooey red sauce on the floor. "I'm full of ideas of what they say to each other, what they do, how they look at each other." He leaned into Jaye and batted his eyelashes.

"Does the guy in the story act as if he's bigger and taller when the girl he likes is around?" Jaye asked. She looked at Jonah and raised her eyebrows. "Does he get all blushy if she's nice to him? Does he have a stupid smile on his face and trip over his own feet?"

Jonah stopped breathing. He wondered if a person's face could actually burst into flames. He hopped off his stool, snatched a paper towel, and busied himself wiping the chili from the floor.

Uncle Nate laughed. "Excellent!" he exclaimed, pinching Jaye's cheek with his free hand. "I can use that." He put down the ladle and grabbed his notebook.

Jaye was all smiles. Jonah could hardly stand it. He was going to set her straight once and for all. She was not coming out on the pond with him again.

"I'll take Jaye to the park, Uncle Nate," he said. "You can stay here and work in peace and quiet." He forced a smile. "Let's go, Jaye."

* * *

"Want to go on the swings?" Jaye asked when they got to the park.

"No."

Jaye shrugged and sat down in one of the swings, pushing herself back and forth with her toe.

Jonah marched to the jungle gym and climbed to the top. After a few minutes of silence, he climbed back down.

He stood in front of Jaye and held the swing chains still. "You have to go back to swim team," he said, trying to keep his voice calm.

Jaye's face crumpled. "I can't go back there," she moaned. "I can't. That kid Gil...the big one from the beach...he's really mean."

"Look, Jaye—" Jonah began.

"No." She shook her head and scrubbed away a tear with the back of her hand. "He told me I better not swim fast or else. He said I'm messing up his times."

A group of kids rode up on bicycles. The girls ran over and draped themselves on the jungle gym facing the swings. Two boys walked toward Jonah and Jaye.

"That's him," Jaye whispered. "The big one is Gil." She grabbed Jonah's hand. "Let's go."

Jonah stepped in front her and waited.

The two boys stopped. Gil stared past Jonah toward the salt pond.

The other boy jerked his chin toward Jaye. "That your sister?"

"Yup," Jonah said.

The kid shoved Gil with his elbow. "Gil here has something he wants to tell her." He looked at Gil. "Go ahead." He poked him again.

"Whatever you have to say, say it to me," Jonah said.

"Sorry," Gil muttered.

The girls shifted on the jungle gym, leaning closer.

"What?" Jonah said. "Didn't hear you."

"Sorry," the big boy said. "All right? I'm *sorry*." He dug a hole in the dirt with the toe of his sneaker. "I was just joking with her."

"Ha ha," Jonah said.

"We had practice heats with another team today," the smaller boy said. "We stunk in the butterfly."

"If I don't get her back, the rest of the team'll kick me off." Gil made a face. "Then my dad'll hit the roof."

"So you're not going to give my sister any more trouble?" Jonah asked.

"Nah," Gil said. He looked down into the tunnel he was digging to China.

"And no one is going to call her KJ anymore?"

The shorter boy shrugged. "Other kids on the team aren't twelve."

The girls on the jungle gym giggled a little.

"Well, it's up to her whether she helps you out or not," Jonah told them. He felt Jaye squeeze his hand. He turned to her.

"I want to go back to the team," she said softly.

"Tomorrow?" he asked.

She nodded.

"Okay, then," Jonah said to the boys. "She'll be there."

Gil filled his cheeks with air and blew out a long breath.

Jonah and Jaye walked to their bikes. They were both smiling.

"See you tomorrow, Jaye," one of the girls called.

"You know something?" Jaye said, turning to Jonah. "I think you *are* bigger and taller than you used to be."

Looks like things might finally be working out, Jonah thought, still smiling.

CHAPTER 23

"You sure you're all right?" Jonah asked Jaye the next afternoon.

"It's okay," she told him. "You can go."

Jonah watched his sister walk across the town beach, her towel slung around her neck. He frowned. It was a gray day, and the water looked a little choppy.

"Jaye!" Two girls ran over and walked Jaye down to the water. They huddled close, one on each side whispering and gesturing. Jaye glanced over her shoulder and sent Jonah a smile.

It's going to be okay, after all, Jonah thought. He hopped on his bike and rode over to the marina.

"Good," Sumi said when he got there. "You're not late."

Once a watch-checker, always a watch-checker, Jonah thought.

She stowed extra clothes and a thermos in the wooden box on the workboat.

"I brought tea in case we get cold and wet, like yesterday," she said.

Jonah wasn't planning on getting wet today or any day. She can have all of the tea, he thought.

Sumi held up a cone of fine netting attached to a metal ring. It was the same size as the air filter in Jonah's parents' station wagon.

"After we check the spat collectors," she said, "we'll tow this net to see if there are any larvae swimming in the water yet." She stowed the net in the wooden box. "Oh, and remind me when we come in—I've got your paycheck through Wednesday in the van." She held a hair band in her teeth and pulled her hair into a ponytail. "It's a good chunk of money," she said, talking around the hair band like Bert did with his cigar, "but I'd pay you twice as much if it were up to me." She slipped the band around her ponytail and tugged it into place.

Jonah checked the gas. He cast off and took them out of the marina, speeding across the pond to the study site. The hull pounded in the chop. Sumi went forward and put her hand on the bow. He saw her touch the lead soldier.

Jonah cut the motor back well before the area of the spat collectors, making sure to give the boat a good ride on its wake. Sumi clung to the gunwale and laughed out loud. Jonah smiled.

He pulled the boat up to the spat collectors, one by one. Sumi leaned way out, bracing her bare legs against the winch as she checked the lines and moorings.

You're really great, she had said to him the day before. He felt something like a little butterfly valve flip in his chest. He thought about how she'd looked at him the day he'd finished up on the Evinrude—like she thought he could do anything. How she left him completely in charge of running their boat. The way she laughed with him now.

What would she say, Jonah wondered darkly, if she

knew I was a liar and a letter thief? He tried not to think about that and concentrated on keeping the workboat in position.

Sumi stood up straight and stretched her back. "Done. They're all perfect." She wiped her hands on her shorts. "Great driving—that's what I call teamwork. Now for the larvae."

She took the cone-shaped net out of the wooden box and clipped its tow wires to the line running out from the winch. "We'll be checking the water column for scallop larvae from now on," she told Jonah. "When we find larvae in the water, we'll know to look for them settling onto the collectors about a week later."

She pulled the winch line through the davit's big wooden pulley. Then she untied the davit arm and swung it out over the water.

"Won't the net catch fish?" Jonah asked.

"This net is designed so it won't really catch much besides the small stuff," Sumi said. The davit's metal arm lurched inboard, then outboard, until she made it fast in the outboard towing position. The net dangled wildly on its clip.

"I'll set the net," Sumi said. "Just try to hold our position until I tell you to move out." She reached for the switch on the winch, then stopped. "I know this will kill you, but we have to go slow when we're towing." She grinned, then let the winch line play out.

Jonah worked the throttle to keep the boat steady. He watched Sumi handle the net, her strong fingers balancing it into the wind until she let it go down and break the surface of the rough water.

"Go ahead," she instructed.

Jonah inched the throttle forward. The motor's hum grew louder. The winch's drum spun slowly. Sumi kept her eye on the line, stopping the winch when the net was fifty feet behind the boat.

"Steady as she goes, cap'n," Sumi called.

Jonah faced forward, handling the throttle as if it were an extension of his own fingers. He controlled their speed and direction easily, despite the waves.

I can do anything, he thought. I can write Mr. Ritchie's stupid story—why not? I can even graduate from high school early. Then I'll go to college where Sumi goes to grad school. *Teamwork,* she'd said. They were a team. Jonah would run the boats—bigger and bigger boats—

"I'm pulling in the net," Sumi announced, interrupting Jonah's thoughts.

He felt the tug of the net on the boat as Sumi reversed the winch and began winding the line back onto the drum. He slowed the motor.

"Get the bucket," she told him.

The net rose out of the water and hung over the side of the boat. Sumi untied the davit, catching the metal arm in time to prevent it from hitting her in the head. She swung it inboard.

What do scallop larvae look like? Jonah wondered. He cut the motor and peered over the rim of the net. He held it steady with the tip of his finger, not wanting to touch the blob of orange and purple goo clinging to the outside of the net.

As Sumi ducked to fasten the davit's rope around the

cleat, they drifted across the wind, and chop caught the workboat broadside. Jonah's finger slipped and the net swung into his face.

He felt a shock, then a burn of fire and ice spread across his lips and cheek. Gasping, he put his hands to his face. He felt something slippery on his cheek and yanked his hands back. He spun away from the net, unable to get any air in his lungs.

"Jonah!" Sumi cried. She tugged on his arm, trying to get him to face her. "What happened? Are you all right?"

Jonah still couldn't breathe. Pain seared his face. His eyes were tearing up. He pulled away from her.

"Stand still." Sumi grabbed his shoulder, but he wrenched free.

"Jonah!" Sumi said sharply. "You have to calm down so I can help you. Try to take some deep breaths." She caught his arm and forced him to sit down on the wooden box.

Jonah gulped for air.

"Oh, no!" she said. "You've been stung by that lion's mane jellyfish!"

Jellyfish? Jonah's stomach twisted into knots.

"Lean out over the side," Sumi commanded. She grabbed a bucket and put her hand on Jonah's back.

Did she think he was going to throw up like he had in Florida? Jonah's breathing was rapid and shallow. He was shivering. He felt like he might pass out, and closed his eyes.

Cold seawater doused his face. He wrenched away from Sumi, coughing.

"Sorry," she said. "It's best to wash away the stinging

cells with seawater." She took out the first aid kit. "Sit back down so I can take the tentacles off."

"N-no m-more seawater!" Jonah sputtered.

"Okay," Sumi said.

He sat down again. Jonah fought the urge to claw at his face as Sumi began to pull the stringy globs off with tweezers. He tried not to shift away from her each time he saw her hand come near.

"You have to stay still," Sumi said. "In your head, try to count to three as you breathe in, then three as you breathe out." She struggled to keep her hands steady as the boat rocked in the waves.

Jonah tried to focus on the numbers. One...two...three. One...two...three. He fought his own panic.

"Keep counting," Sumi said. "Good." She continued to work with the tweezers. "There, I think that's it," she said finally. "That was a pretty big bunch of tentacles." She held up a stringy tangle.

"I don't want to see that!" Jonah jerked away from her.

"It's okay, Jonah," Sumi said. She put the tentacles into a plastic bag and sealed it. "See? I'm not even going to throw them back in the water. You're safe."

"It's never safe." Jonah shuddered.

"What do you mean?" Sumi asked. "What's going on, Jonah?"

"Last year in Florida..." He stopped talking to pull in a deep breath. "Last year I got stung by a Portuguese man-of-war...it was really bad...I had to go to the hospital. That's why I don't go in water like this. And I never will!"

Sumi sat down on the box next to him. "That's terrible.

Anybody would be afraid of getting stung again if they'd had a scare like that," she said. She took out her thermos and poured steaming tea onto the corner of a towel. "This may seem weird, but heat is supposed to do the trick. Here now, close your eyes."

She cupped his chin with her hand and held the tea-soaked towel against his face. She was very gentle. After a few minutes, the fire in his lip and cheek subsided, and Jonah felt himself relax. He stopped shaking. Sumi was close and he picked up the scent of her hair as it brushed his neck.

"Any better?" she asked.

He liked the touch of her hands on his face. "A little," he said.

She poured more tea onto the towel. Jonah closed his eyes as she pressed the hot cloth to his lip and cheek. Sumi hadn't made fun of him for being afraid. Jonah felt as if he could trust her with anything. Maybe he should tell her about his other troubles, too, like lying to Uncle Nate about where he was in the afternoons. About stealing the letter.

There was a thump under the hull. Jonah opened his eyes and saw that the wind had forced the workboat almost onto the barrier beach.

"Lucky we ran aground," Sumi said. "We were drifting toward the breachway."

Jonah stood up to go reverse the motor. His legs were still shaky.

"I'll get it," Sumi said. "You sit and dab your sting with this tea." She soaked the towel again and gave it to him.

Then she went to the console and started the motor. She looked up at him, laughing.

"What?" Jonah called to her over the motor and the wind. What was so funny? His lips felt rubbery and numb.

Sumi cupped her hands to her mouth. "Wait until the kids get a look at your fat lip—you won't be able to kiss your little girlfriends for weeks!" She laughed again and reached for the throttle.

Jonah stared at her in horror. Her words stung deeper than any jellyfish could. *Little girlfriends?* After everything, how could she think of him as just a kid? "Don't say that!" he shouted at her, dropping the towel.

Sumi gave him a bewildered look. "Jonah," she said. She started toward him. "I didn't—"

In two steps Jonah was in the bow, then over the gunwale. From the beach he heaved the workboat off the sand with his shoulder.

"Jonah, wait!" Sumi cried.

But he was already pounding down the barrier beach as fast as he could run.

CHAPTER 24

Saturday afternoon's sky was gun gray. Jonah tossed the oars in the skiff and pushed away from the dock. Uncle Nate had been half asleep on the couch when Jonah had gone out the door. But he'd told his uncle he was going out on the pond, and that was rule number one. As for the other rule, well, Jonah wasn't going anywhere near the breachway. He wasn't even going to look at that side of the salt pond. Why would he want to be near that stupid study site, anyway? And why did it feel like he had a dead spark plug lodged in his chest?

He started to row across the pond toward the cove and Bert's marina. He'd get the Evinrude hooked onto his skiff and it would be as great as he'd always thought it would be. A light wind filled Jonah's ears. Sporadic raindrops dotted the pond's rough surface. The collage of white and gray clouds mixed and broke apart overhead.

It was hard rowing. Jonah was glad that Jaye hadn't wanted to come. She was waiting for the clouds to blow over so Uncle Nate could take her to the beach. Jonah rested a moment to wipe his face with the bottom of his T-shirt, moving his fingers gingerly around his swollen lip.

He hoped Lenny and Al would be somewhere else today.

Jonah heard a shout and looked back. Uncle Nate was on the end of the dock jumping up and down. What a send-off, Jonah thought. Uncle Nate's long arms and legs shot up into the air at all angles. Jonah smiled a little, remembering what his uncle had said about his lip.

"Don't tell me," Uncle Nate had said the night before. "Pliers that needed to be taught a lesson? A hammer that just wouldn't toe the line?"

It had hurt to smile. "Stop, Uncle Nate," Jonah had said, his words coming out more like "Stah, Unca Nay."

"That fat lip looks cool, Jonah," Jaye had said. She'd won three races at a swim meet and had been hoisted up on her teammates' shoulders to celebrate. Jonah could do no wrong as far as she was concerned.

Jonah waved to his uncle on the dock, then pulled his hand back. Oh, so what, he thought. Waving didn't always mean you were in trouble. Maybe Uncle Nate was just excited about how he'd fixed up the skiff. If he liked that, just wait until he saw the Evinrude! Jonah was going to tell his uncle that he was borrowing the motor. No need to mention who from, though. Uncle Nate was so preoccupied with his book he probably wouldn't ask any more questions. Jonah glanced around the skiff. Uh-oh, he thought. Was Uncle Nate waving because the life vest was still sitting on the dock? Too late now. Jonah would have to borrow another one from Bert for the trip back across.

It took a lot longer than Jonah had thought it would to row to the marina. He pulled the skiff up on the beach and went into the store. The place was dark and empty, except for a halo of cigar smoke near the back.

"Figured you'd show, weather brewin' or no." Bert was sitting in a folding chair at the end of the counter. He stood up. "Let's get her hooked up quick so's you kin get ba—"

The old man stopped and peered at Jonah's face. He let out a low whistle.

Jonah shifted from foot to foot. "Jellyfish," he mumbled.

"When you were out with Sumi yesterday?"

"Yeah."

"Coulda been lots worse," Bert said.

No, Jonah thought, yesterday could not have been much worse. He looked at the floor and blew out a sigh. Bert eyed him another moment, then went to the cash register and hit a button. The register made a loud ding. He held out a piece of paper. "She left this for you."

It was Jonah's paycheck, issued by the college in the amount of one hundred and sixty dollars. That was a lot of money, but he still didn't have enough for the Evinrude. He knew it, and Bert knew it, too. Jonah crumpled the check into his pocket.

The old man helped Jonah carry the motor from the lean-to down to the skiff. He went to get some extra parts from the storeroom, then helped Jonah hook up the motor. Jonah tossed in a life jacket.

"You kin borrow this gas can," Bert said, "for the time bein'." He took his cigar out and spat to the side, staring across the cove. He rubbed his head through his knitted cap. "Look here," he said finally. "I'll have to ask you to bring it back when someone wants to look it over."

Jonah barely managed a nod.

He shoved his skiff into the water and pulled it along

the dock by its rope so he could step in. He held his breath, crossed his fingers, and pull-started the Evinrude. It gave a weak cough. Jonah's breath caught in his throat. He looked up at Bert in alarm.

"It's been outta commission a good long time." Bert jerked his chin at the pull cord. "Give it another go."

Three more "go's" and the Evinrude roared to life. Jonah wiped his oily hands on his shirt.

"You're a quick study, tell you what," Bert said.

Jonah cast off his line and wound his skiff through the maze of docks and moored boats. He sat in the stern, getting the feel of having a throttle and tiller on one handle. If he pushed the tiller to the right, the bow moved left. He swung the tiller back and forth and twisted the throttle until he got the hang of it.

"Wind's really pickin' up. Storm's comin' on quicker than I thought," Bert called. He had his hand on his cap, and his flannel shirt billowed around him. "Extra strong tide's goin' out, too. Head right home, an' hug the shore. No toolin' around. I'm gonna call your uncle an' let him know you're on your way."

Jonah nodded to Bert, then headed for the mouth of the cove. He opened the throttle and the bow rose. It didn't exactly fly like the Whaler, but it felt good. It felt great. Jonah gripped the Evinrude's tiller and ran his other hand over the patch in the skiff's hull.

"I'm Boat Guy!" he yelled into the wind.

I'll have to ask you to bring it back.

"Boat Guy," Jonah whispered.

* * *

A seagull tossed by above the skiff, its feathers ragged in the wind. The rain had started in earnest. Jonah hunched his shoulders, trying to keep the chilled drops from going down his neck. The Evinrude worked hard against the rising waves. Bert didn't have to worry, Jonah thought. He wasn't going anywhere except straight home to Uncle Nate's. It was getting late, anyway.

Suddenly Bert's parting words came back to Jonah with a jolt. *I'm gonna call your uncle an' let him know you're on your way.* How did Bert know about Uncle Nate?

As Jonah turned to look back at the marina, his eyes swept the pond. There was the workboat, rocking in the rough water over the study site. What was she doing out there? he wondered.

The workboat looked empty. Jonah shrugged. Why should he care if some college girl was stupid enough to come out in a storm? He noticed that the anchor line was out, but the boat seemed to be drifting anyway.

A dark head appeared. Sumi had been hidden behind the boat's motor. Jonah strained to listen through the rain and wind. He couldn't make out any engine sound. Sumi bent next to the motor again, then reappeared.

She waved to him, a small figure all in black. Her wet suit, Jonah guessed. He thought about the first day he'd seen her waving at him from the workboat. She'd been at the other end of the pond, near the sandbar. Jonah looked away. He didn't have to wave to her if he didn't want to. He kept motoring toward Uncle Nate's. He tried not to look back at Sumi again, but he couldn't help it. She was still waving. *Waving,* he realized with a shock. The signal for trouble!

Jonah turned his skiff toward the study site. The workboat had drifted away from the shallow area and was dragging its anchor into the channel near the breachway. What was wrong with her motor? Jonah fought the current and waves to reach the workboat. He tied up with the line Sumi threw to him.

"It's the motor," she yelled. The wind whipped wet hair across her mouth and she pushed it away. "It just quit on me and I can't get it to start—and the walkie-talkie's not working!"

Jonah's foot slipped as he climbed across the gunwales. He looked down into the roiling, murky water, then heaved himself into the workboat.

Sumi moved away to give him room near the motor. He checked all of the connections. Waves slapped the boats broadside, sending spray high in the air. Sumi scrambled to secure loose gear. Jonah shook the gas can. It felt full. He reached for the priming bulb on the tank's connecting hose. The hard rubber bulb had collapsed in on itself like a deflated balloon. There was no air in there—that was a vapor lock. He checked the tank again. The small air vent at the top of the tank was plugged with a wad of pink bubblegum. Lenny was always chewing gum!

"Lenny did this!" Jonah shouted. He pried the gum away with his fingers. "I got it!" He reached for the priming bulb.

A wave slammed into the side of the workboat. Jonah lost his footing and careened into the wooden box. A sharp pain shot through his ribs. As he pulled himself up, he noticed that the rope securing the davit had come loose.

Another wave hit the boat, and the davit swung across the deck in a wide arc.

"Look out!" Jonah yelled.

The heavy wooden pulley caught Sumi in the back of the head and knocked her overboard.

"Sumi!" Jonah cried. She didn't answer. He kicked off his sneakers and dove into the heaving water.

CHAPTER 25

Jonah plowed through the whitecaps, the water washing over his head. Sumi bobbed on her back, her wet suit keeping her afloat. When he reached her, Jonah grabbed her arm and shook her.

"Sumi," he yelled. A wave slapped into his mouth. He spat out cold, salty water. "Sumi!"

Her eyes were closed. Jonah held her under her arm, treading water. He put his other hand in front of her nose and mouth. He could feel her warm breath on his palm. She was alive!

Rain pelted Jonah's head and face. The outgoing tide pushed them toward the breachway. Water churned in angry currents. Spray from waves outside of the barrier beach shot over the stone retaining walls. Jonah kicked and flailed. The boats were ahead of him, already at the breachway's opening. In another minute they would enter the narrow channel, caroming off the rough stone walls like some grisly game of pinball. Soon the Evinrude, his patched skiff, and the workboat would all be reduced to splinters. The splinters would be tumbled under the waves and washed out to sea.

A sob wracked Jonah's chest. The boats disappeared behind a curve in the wall. Did it even matter, he thought? When Uncle Nate found out what Jonah had done, and what he'd been doing all summer, Jonah wouldn't get near the skiff—or any other boat—for the rest of his life.

He readjusted his grip on Sumi, reaching across her chest and catching her under her other arm. He kicked hard against the pull of the tide. They were still drifting into the breachway. His efforts seemed futile against the force of the water. When he and his friends had carried each other around the swimming pool, it had seemed almost silly. What good was his lifesaving class now?

Jonah struggled to get them away from the breachway. Swimming against the current was using up all of his strength. Maybe if he swam across the current instead of against it, they'd have a chance. If he couldn't, they would be swept into the frothing channel, sucked under a riptide, and shot out to sea.

Jonah aimed for the inner shore of the empty barrier beach, just east of the breachway's opening. He thrashed at the water with his free arm and scissored his legs harder than he'd ever thought he could. Sumi's head jerked back and forth as he pulled her with him. He fought his way across the current, stroke by stroke. He knew he couldn't stop to rest. Jonah pulled and kicked with all his might. His toe grazed sloping sand and he lunged toward shore.

He found himself in choppy water, chest-deep. He was standing. He was out of the channel, and near enough to shore to be free of the tidal current. They were going to make it.

Sumi floated on her back as he pulled her across the shallows. Hooking his hands under her arms, he hauled her up onto the shore. His heels ground holes in the wet sand on the short beach. When they were away from the water, he let go of Sumi and collapsed next to her, gulping air.

Sumi lay motionless on the rough beach grass. Her eyelids fluttered. Jonah pushed her onto her side. He thumped between her shoulder blades with the heel of his hand. She stirred, then heaved up onto one elbow and turned away, coughing and retching.

"Sumi!" Jonah cried. "Are you all right?"

She raised one arm. Her slender hand shook as she patted the top of her head once, twice, three times. She was okay. Jonah shut his eyes and turned to the sky, letting the rain wash the saltwater off his face.

Above the drumming of the rain, Jonah heard the roar of a large motorboat.

"Can—" Sumi coughed. She sat up. "Can they see us?" She pushed dark strings of hair out of her eyes.

Jonah got to his feet and scanned the pond. The clouds were beginning to break up. A fishing boat approached. Jonah waved to the boat, swinging his arm wide. He was in trouble, all right. And was he ever glad to see help on the way. After a long minute, the wheelhouse was visible. Then Jonah saw who was steering the boat. He shrank back against the sand, pulling Sumi by her shoulder.

"It's Lenny!" he said. "Stay down!"

Wasn't sabotaging Sumi's boat enough? Jonah thought. He looked around in a panic. The beach grass was too sparse to hide them. If they got up to run, Lenny would see them for sure. Jonah lay there as still as he could. The motor sound grew louder. Then it started to fade.

Jonah tipped his head up for a look. The boat had passed them. It headed into the breachway. He's going after our boats, Jonah thought with a sinking heart. If he'd had any hope of the boats surviving the breachway, he knew now that he'd never see them again.

"That's it," he said, almost to himself. He put his face in his hands.

"No, look," Sumi said after a few minutes. Her voice was weak. She sat up, pointing toward the mouth of the breachway.

The bow of Lenny's boat reappeared from behind the stone wall. Its progress was slow. They watched the fishing boat lumber out of the channel. The motor sounded loud and uneven, like it was straining. A tow cable stretched back from the fishing boat's powerful winch. Jonah couldn't believe what he was seeing. Behind Lenny's boat, the workboat and Jonah's skiff rocked into view. They were both whole and sound. Lenny was heading toward the marina. Jonah leaped to his feet.

"Jonah!" A man's voice shouted his name.

Jonah whipped around. Uncle Nate towered above him on the dunes.

* * *

In two long bounds Uncle Nate was by Jonah's side, gripping him by the shoulders. For a second Jonah wasn't sure if his uncle meant to hug him or shake him.

"You really gave us a scare, Toolboy," Uncle Nate said.

"Thank goodness you're okay."

Jaye waved from the crest of the dunes. "I have blankets," she called.

"Whoa, there!" Uncle Nate exclaimed. He stepped past Jonah and caught Sumi, who was swaying unsteadily to her feet. "Sumi, is it? Here, let me help you up." He put her arm around his neck and turned to Jonah. "Can you make it?"

Jonah nodded. Jaye ran down to him and put the blanket on his shoulders.

"We saw you in the water from way over there," she said, pointing to the end of the barrier beach. "Wow! I want to take lifesaving, too."

Uncle Nate wrapped Sumi in a blanket and helped her over the dunes. On the other side, Al's red truck sat idling.

Jonah drew back. "A-Al?" he said through chattering teeth.

"Al didn't do any of this, Jonah," Uncle Nate said.

Jonah tried to get his mind around that as he stumbled down the slope of the dunes.

"Here, now," Al said, when they reached the truck. He opened the doors. "Let's get those two out of this wind."

Jonah's whole body shook. Uncle Nate helped Sumi into the front of the truck next to Al. He waited while Jonah crawled into the narrow rear seat with Jaye, then got in and slammed the door.

They bumped over the wet sand. The last of the rain spit at the windshield as the storm blew over. Al turned the heat on full blast. The wipers squeaked a steady rhythm, and no one talked. Little by little Jonah's shaking subsided. His muscles felt like lead weights. Jaye slipped her hand in his. Jonah stopped fighting to stay awake and let himself slump over onto the seat.

I was in that water a long time, he thought. His eyes closed, and he relaxed. I was in the water and I'm okay. I'm really okay.

CHAPTER 26

The smell of cocoa wafted past Jonah's nose. Morning sun streamed in the picture window, bathing the couch in buttery warmth. Jonah blinked and looked around. What was he doing sleeping in the living room? Jonah scratched his head. His hair felt stiff and sticky.

Memories of the day before flooded back—watching in horror as Sumi fell overboard, fighting through the waves to the barrier beach, seeing Lenny towing the boats. *Lenny!*

Jonah sat up and groaned. His whole body ached. He vaguely remembered getting out of Al's truck and stumbling into the cabin. Uncle Nate had left again with Al to…to do what? Jonah screwed his eyes shut and thought hard. To take Sumi and her van back to the college. Jaye had stayed here. His little sister had gotten him a dry T-shirt and sweatpants. She'd given him hot soup and had tucked a quilt around him when he couldn't keep his eyes open.

"I'd say you earned that sleep." Uncle Nate came in and handed Jonah a steaming mug. "Feel up to a little Uncle-to-Toolboy talk?" He sat and stretched his long legs out, resting his feet on the coffee table. He looked at Jonah and took a sip from his own mug of cocoa.

"Is Sumi okay?" Jonah asked.

"Sumi is just fine. After we dropped you off, we all had a long talk at Bert's. Then I drove her back up to the college in her van. Al followed in his truck so he could bring me home."

Jonah sighed. He noticed that the cabin was unusually quiet. He glanced over his shoulder toward the doorway of his room and asked, "Where's Jaye?"

"A friend of hers from swim team came by and asked her to go to the park. You know the swim team, don't you? The swim team that Jaye's too young for, but swims with because she's impersonating you?"

Jonah sloshed cocoa as he set his mug on the coffee table. "Uncle Nate—"

"That swim team," Uncle Nate continued, "that practices in a salt pond?" He stood up and began to pace. "Did you know how you were going to feel about open water before you got here?"

"Not really. But—"

"I'm sure your parents had no idea, either. But as soon as you got here, you told me you only swam in pools," Uncle Nate went on, "and I didn't pay enough attention." He rapped his knuckles against his head. "Good thing Bert called me the day you showed up on his doorstep. Or should I say the day you 'broke' the already broken power pack?"

"Already broken?" Jonah didn't know whether to laugh or cry. He felt like he was still being tossed around by the waves. "You knew I wasn't on the swim team the whole

173

time? But wait—how did Bert even know who I was?"

"This is a small town," Uncle Nate said. "Everybody knows everybody. Folks watch out for each other, like Bert was watching out for you. I was sure you'd tell me about it when you were ready. But you never did. And everything could have turned out a whole lot worse yesterday if I really hadn't known what you were up to." He raised his eyebrows and looked at Jonah.

Jonah put his head in his hands. "I was trying not to bother you," he said to his feet. "You needed to work on your book. I'm really sorry I lied to you, Uncle Nate."

"Here's the thing," his uncle said. He leaned forward and put a hand on Jonah's shoulder. "There's nothing more important to me than you and Jaye, Toolboy. It's that love thing. That's what uncles are for." He gave Jonah's shoulder a gentle shake.

Jonah thought about the letter from school, crumpled in the back of the bureau drawer. "Uncle Nate," he whispered.

His uncle didn't seem to have heard him. "You know," he continued, walking over to gaze out the picture window, "your parents are due back next weekend. If I'm storing your boat until next summer, you're going to have to tell me how to take care of it."

Jonah looked at his uncle's back. "Next summer? But I thought you were going to rent the place out. Don't you have to work? Anyway, the motor's not mine, and it's not going to be. It costs too much money." His words caught in his throat.

They heard a noisy truck pull into the driveway.

"Kin I get a look at Rip van Winkle?" The back screen

door creaked open, then shut with a bang. Bert ambled into the living room and peered out from under his bushy eyebrows at Jonah.

"How's the kid?"

"Not much worse for wear." Uncle Nate smiled.

"More'n I kin say for Lenny." Bert let out a bark of a laugh. "He might be in better shape if Sumi did press charges, after all. Al hollered at him up and down the store, out to the truck, and all the way home, far's I kin tell. Lenny's ears'll be ringing for a month. He's gotta pay damages an' do repairs for Sumi. I'm givin' him chores, too—real good ones." Bert rubbed his stubby hands together.

"Chores!" Jonah burst out. "We almost drowned!"

"That's true, but Lenny didn't mean for that part to happen," Bert said.

"What part didn't he mean?" Jonah fumed. "The 'almost' part?"

"He didn't mean the harm part of it," Bert said. "Len was just tryin' to set Sumi back a bit. The water in the gas, clipping them plastic rings, the bubblegum." Bert shook his head. "Bubblegum! He was hopin' she'd cut her losses an' pack up before scallop season. Thought gettin' her off the pond was what his pop wanted. You shoulda seen Al's face when he heard that!" Bert rolled his eyes and whistled.

"Lenny didn't think Sumi would go out on a Saturday," Uncle Nate continued the explanation. "He expected the motor to stall out on Monday, when you would be there to help her."

"He didn't break that radio, neither," Bert added. "That's just a piece of junk."

"I talked to him, Jonah, and Lenny is really very upset. He's so sorry," Uncle Nate said. "Now he and his dad both understand that Sumi's work might eventually help the scallops. It's no excuse for what Lenny did, but times have been tough for fishermen around here, lately, haven't they, Bert?"

"Not so great for my marina, either," Bert said. "Least I've found someone to take that Evinrude offa my hands."

"Oh yeah?" Uncle Nate asked.

Jonah thought he might burst into tears.

"What do you think of that face, Bert?" Uncle Nate pointed at Jonah.

"Don't he want it?" Bert asked. Extra creases appeared around his ice blue eyes.

Jonah looked from Bert to Uncle Nate and back again. He held his breath.

"Jonah, remember when I was waving to you from the dock yesterday?" Uncle Nate said. "When you took off in your skiff? I was trying to tell you something." He stopped and looked at Jonah. "Well, two somethings."

"Was one about the life jacket?" Jonah said, grimacing.

"Yes. But the other thing was the most absolutely stupendous news—"

"Your uncle got writin' money!" Bert cut in.

Uncle Nate pulled a piece of paper off of the kitchen counter. "I got a grant." He waved the paper. "A work-in-progress grant. The grant committee liked the beginning of my book! I can use this money to come back here next summer and finish. No more rushing it."

"That's great, Uncle Nate," Jonah said. "Really great. I mean it. I just don't get what that has to do with—"

"Well, if he's comin', then you're comin' back here to work for me next summer, that's what," Bert said. "I got better things to do than spend my time takin' that Evinrude back offa your skiff. You kin work off the rest of the money. I kin use a good boat guy."

Jonah felt he must be grinning from head to toe, but he wasn't sure his fat lip was participating. "Sure," he said. "Yeah, sure. I mean, if my parents say yes."

"Right. Well, I gotta get back," Bert said. "Just wanted to check in."

"Hey, thanks for everything, Bert." Uncle Nate shook his hand.

"Yeah," Jonah stood and held out his hand to Bert. "Thanks. Thanks a lot."

The old man gripped Jonah's hand between both of his like a vise. Then he turned and stumped out of the cabin. The door banged behind him.

"One of a kind," Uncle Nate said.

They heard Bert's truck drive away down the road.

"I definitely want to work at the marina next summer, but I can pay for a lot of the motor now," Jonah told him. "I've got a paycheck, and money saved besides."

"Why don't you hang onto some of that money, Toolboy? Put it aside for engineering school," Uncle Nate said. "I know you'll probably get a full scholarship, but you always need extra money for books, or wrenches and pliers, or whatever they use there." He smiled.

Engineering school? Jonah thought. He slumped back down onto the couch. I'm not even going to make it past seventh-grade English.

Uncle Nate eyed him curiously. "What? Did I say something wrong?"

Another engine rumbled in the driveway. There was a knock at the door.

"Hello?" It was Sumi's voice.

Jonah froze.

Uncle Nate looked at Jonah's face. "I'll get it," he said.

Jonah heard the murmur of their voices outside. After a minute, Uncle Nate came back into the room.

"The scallop larvae aren't swimming in the water yet, so Sumi's going home to California for a visit. She came to say good-bye."

Jonah wasn't sure he could face her. Sumi probably knew by now that he'd lied, and that he wasn't even supposed to be working at Bert's in the first place. And what if she said something to him about what had happened that last workday—the day he'd jumped ship? Jonah couldn't bear that.

"I think she's kind of in a hurry," Uncle Nate said. "She's got a plane to catch. She's waiting for you by the van. So go."

Jonah rose to his feet and trudged out the back door. Sumi was leaning against a tree, hands behind her back. Her long dark hair shone almost blue where the sun found it through the leaves. She smiled at him.

Jonah looked at the ground. "My uncle says you're leaving," he mumbled.

"Just a quick visit home. You're going home, too, right?"

"End of the week."

"I want to thank you, Jonah," Sumi said, "and not just for pulling me to shore. I'm really grateful to you for helping me set up my study. I don't think I could have gotten my work done without you this summer. No." She shook her head. "I *know* I couldn't have."

Jonah dug in the dirt with his bare toe.

"Everybody has things they know, and things they need to learn," she continued. "I learned a lot from you."

Jonah concentrated on the hole he was digging as if it were a highly technical construction project. He wondered what shade of red his face had turned. Gas can red? Al's truck red?

"You know, most people are afraid of something," Sumi said. "But it's how you face your fears that makes all the difference."

Jonah couldn't look straight at her. With the corner of his eye he saw Sumi bring her hands out from behind her back.

"I brought you this," she said. "Here." She held out her hand. In it was the lead soldier.

Jonah shook his head. "You should keep him in the boat. You need him. He's your hero, remember?"

"Not even close." Sumi took Jonah's hand and pressed the soldier into it. "I have a real hero now."

Jonah watched her climb into the blue van. He lifted his hand to wave good-bye. When she was gone, he put his hand to his cheek to touch the kiss she'd left behind.

Chapter 27

Jonah went straight to his room and got the letter from Mr. Ritchie. He handed it to Uncle Nate.

Uncle Nate read and reread the letter. He scratched his head.

"Clue me in," he said finally. Jonah could see his uncle working hard not to smile. "Where's the *real* problem?"

"Uncle Nate, this *is* the real problem." Jonah crossed his arms. "It's not funny. I'm going to be in remedial English next year—if I live that long."

Jaye came in the back door and pulled off her bicycle helmet. She looked at the letter in Uncle Nate's hands.

"I showed him," Jonah said to his sister.

"What do you mean, if you live that long?" Uncle Nate asked.

"Did you tell him that Mom and Dad don't know about it?" Jaye said to Jonah.

His uncle whistled. "They don't know about this letter from your teacher?"

Jonah hung his head. "I was afraid they wouldn't let me come here if they knew," he said. "I took the letter. It was so stupid. Instead of helping, it ruined everything. And now they probably won't let me come back next summer, either."

"They might not, Jonah," Uncle Nate said. "But then again, they might. It depends on a lot of things. One thing you have on your side is their vacation."

"Their vacation?" Jonah repeated.

"They've been having a blast in Europe for weeks. They're relaxed, refreshed, and they've missed you."

"I've missed them," Jaye said.

"Me, too," Jonah admitted.

"The other thing you have on your side is your fabulous and well-written story."

"You finished your story?" Jaye asked.

"No. That's the problem, Uncle Nate," Jonah said. "There is no story."

"Sure there is." Uncle Nate tapped Jonah's forehead. "It's all right in there. And you've got this whole week to get it on paper. You'll have something to show your parents, *and* something to hand in to Mr. Ritchie. Of course, you'll still have to do your time in summer school."

"I know," Jonah groaned. "I know."

"But you need that story for Mr. Ritchie, so let's get started."

Jonah just stared at him, baffled.

"I'll help you get started thinking," Uncle Nate said. "Remember when you first got here, and you told me nothing interesting ever happens to you?" He grinned at Jonah.

"Okay, I was wrong," Jonah said. "Now I've had all the

'interesting' things happen to me that I need for the rest of my life."

"I hope not." Uncle Nate laughed. "But you do have a great story." He gave Jonah a shove. "Go get your journal and start putting it all down on paper."

"Uncle Nate is right," Jaye exclaimed. "That stuff that happened to you out on the pond is a great story. If you do the words, I'll draw the pictures!" She grabbed her journal from the coffee table.

Jonah went to find his own journal. He thought about the night before—the boats, the storm, jumping into the water—could he really write that story?

He sat on the couch and opened the journal. Jaye stretched out on the floor and started to draw. Jonah stared at the empty first page. He hit the paper with the pencil eraser. *Tap, tap, tap.* It made him think about a knocking noise he'd heard in Al's truck. Did Al know what the noise was? Maybe he should go over to the marina later and see if the red truck was there.

Jonah looked up. Uncle Nate was watching him. Jonah sighed.

"I can't get started," he said. "I never can. I start thinking about a project, like motors or something instead. I don't know how to think about writing."

"What do you do when you want to start working on a motor?" Uncle Nate asked.

"Huh?" Jonah gave him a funny look.

"Come on, Uncle Nate, he has to write, not work on motors," Jaye said.

"Humor me here," Uncle Nate said. "When you're working on a Toolboy project, what do you do first?"

Jonah thought. "I guess I make sure I have all of the parts."

"Right!" Uncle Nate hit his palm with his fist. "I do exactly the same thing when I'm writing a story. Only instead of the spark plugs and dragonfly valves, I use—"

"Butterfly valves," Jonah corrected.

"Those too. Instead of those parts, I use a certain place, and some interesting people. Then I put them together and have something happen."

"You mean, like I'd use the salt pond for the place?"

"And boy, something happened all right," Jaye said. "I'm drawing the rescue first!"

Uncle Nate nodded. "And you couldn't invent a better cast of characters."

"But what happened to me—it's all so crazy," Jonah said. "It'll sound like I made it up."

"It's a *story*," Uncle Nate said. "It doesn't have to be true. You can even tell some real parts and make up the rest. Make up a bad guy who's bad through and through. Throw in a little romance."

Jaye giggled.

Jonah's face felt suddenly warm. "No romance," he muttered.

"Sure, sure—leave out the romance." Uncle Nate smiled. "For now."

Jonah looked down at his notebook again. What could he write? *I came to my uncle's pond. I worked for Bert. I had to go into the water. The end.* Jonah shook his head.

"Does a motor start once you've got all of the parts together?" Uncle Nate prompted.

"Well, not without fuel," Jonah said.

"So here." Uncle Nate pointed to the empty page. "Your fuel is going to be the details—the sights, the sounds, the smells, what people say to each other. You know, get the people talking. That's what a story runs on."

"Now you're starting to sound like Mr. Ritchie," Jonah said. "Except for the motor thing."

"See that? Mr. Ritchie's not all bad. Now, not to push that motor thing too far, but what starts the motor running?" Uncle Nate asked. "It's a spark, right?"

"Right," Jonah said.

"So you start your story with something that will grab readers. That's your spark. See if you can come up with one."

Jonah closed his eyes. He thought a long, long time. He wrote. Jaye tried to peek at what he was writing, so he hid his work with his hand. He turned the page and wrote some more. His stomach growled.

"I'll get you two some sandwiches," Uncle Nate said. "You work."

It was work. Hard work. And it was going to take lots more to get the job done. But Jonah thought he just might have good parts for his story, and when he closed his eyes and put himself in the scene, he found lots of fuel. He took a bite of the sandwich Uncle Nate brought him without even looking at it.

I'm going to miss this, he thought, chewing a sticky mouthful of peanut butter and marshmallow fluff. He wiped his mouth with the back of his hand. His swollen lip felt much better. He watched Jaye draw for a minute, then went back to his writing.

"There," he said to Uncle Nate finally. It had taken a long time to write just one paragraph, but it was a start. "How's that for the beginning?" He turned back to the first page and pointed.

Uncle Nate read out loud. "It was a dark and stormy night?" He looked pained. "Jonah—"

"Gotcha!" Jonah laughed. He took the journal back and turned the page.

> *The first day I took the Whaler out, little bits of sun jumped all over the salt pond. The Whaler's Mercury 50 horsepower motor roared, and my ears were full of wind. A seagull raced me, like I was flying, too. I yelled, "I love this pond!" But I knew I had to stay out of the water, and I couldn't tell anyone why.*

Uncle Nate nodded. He smiled, and nodded some more. Then he grabbed the notebook and swatted Jonah over the head.

"Thanks, Uncle Nate," Jonah said, and he beamed, fat lip and all.

LESLIE BULION is the author of several children's books, including TALL SHIPS FUN and FATUMA'S NEW CLOTH, winner of the African Studies Association's 2003 Children's Africana Book Award. She has always loved the sea, and studied oceanography on and in the Rhode Island coastal salt ponds. She lives with her husband, two daughters, and two dogs in Connecticut.